Mafia Princess

and

White Feather

Mafia Princess

and

White Feather

How far will she go

to protect the ones she loves?

What will be left

standing in the end?

Sheila Chandler

Chandler Publishing

2016

First Printing: 2016

ISBN 978-0-578-18239-1

Chandler Publishing
P.O. Box 131
Coward, South Carolina 29530

This book is dedicated to:

Kelvin

Dana

My husband, my best friend…
My beautiful daughter, my angel…
Thank you for believing in me…
Sometimes just believing can make your dreams come true.

I love you both always & forever...

"Does our past define our future?

My legacy is one of power...

There is no greater power than love...

It can bring you to your knees or it can drive you to murder..."

Arabella Marcello

Chapter 1

My name is Arabella Marcello – but everyone calls me Princess and I am the only girl in our Mafia family clan. Just remember everything you ever heard or seen about the Mafia and believe me it is all true.

Killing someone for answers really just seems normal in our family.

I could shoot a gun from the time I was ten years old.

For my tenth birthday my father bought me my first gun – a small shiny pink 22 pistol.

I know I live an odd life but it's my life and I love it…

So let me tell you a little about my Mafia *famiglia* (family).

The Sicilian Mafia – Cosa Nostra as it is sometimes called, is made up of five families going back five generations – originally from Sicily, Italy but now here in America as well.

Only two generations of our clan are still alive.

There are Five Original Clan Heads of the Mafia family:

Victor DeLuca

Carmin Marcello (my father)

John Cardea

Stefano Valachio

Costa Accardo

The five of them along with Benito, are known as the elders. They have changed the Sicilian Mafia from the old ways, to what it is today. All of them used to live in Italy together, in the villa that has been in our families for generations.

The five of them along with John's brother, Benito Cardea created *Nostra Tesorino Winery* (Our Little Treasure Winery).

We sell the number one grape and olive wine in all of Italy – name *Nostra Tesorino Vino* (our little treasure wine).

Now only Victor along with his son Nick lives in Italy at *Tesori Cove Villa* (Treasures Cove Villa).

The rest moved to America a year and a half before I was born and bought a great deal of land.

There was enough land that they built Nostra Tesorino Winery along with four separate towns.

My father Carmin created the town Haven Falls.

John and Benito together built the town Paradise Falls.

Stefano built the town Angels Falls along with Nostra Tesorino Winery. The Winery was placed in the center of the town; where all the grape and olive wine is prepared and bottled.

Costa built the town Angels Paradise, which includes the airstrip and hangers that houses our two planes.

Stefano and Costa live together in the estate they built on the line where their two towns meet.

The elders planted the grape and olive fields on the outskirts of the towns – far away from the homes and shops in each of the four towns.

Over time the four towns grew and now *Nostra Tesorino Vino* is the top selling wine in the US as well as Italy.

I live in Grace Manor in the town of Haven Falls, where my dad is the Sheriff.

John built Sea Court Manor and Benito built Heart Point Manor several miles apart in the town of Paradise Falls.

John is the sheriff of Paradise Falls and his brother Benito is deputy.

As you can see, my father and John may no longer be Head of the Family – but they both are the Head of their towns. Always pretending they are living in some old western walking around always carrying a gun.

Stefano and Costa built Angel Brook Villa where they live together with Carlos – he is their protector or hit-man, as most people would say.

Since neither have any children, I will inherit both towns and the villa, respectively when they die.

My father and the elders built their homes several miles away from the center of the four towns.

As I was saying before – I am Arabella and today's the last day Aaron and I will be living with our parents at Haven Manor.

My brother Aaron and I both are leaving Haven Falls.

We are officially moving to Paradise Falls tomorrow.

My best friend Lily and I graduated from high school yesterday and I am finally getting my new car.

Aaron got it for me as a graduation present but won't tell me what kind it is. My brother really likes surprising me and has been doing it all my life.

Aaron is eighteen and is now Head of the Family – he has taken over for our father Carmin.

In our family, once the first born male turns eighteen he takes his father's place as Head of the Family.

Since I am the only girl in our clan as well as the other two Mafia Clans, I am not sure what will happen with me.

I am turning sixteen in two weeks and I am already heir to Angels Falls and Angels Paradise. I have no freaking clue how to run one town, let alone two!

Thank goodness at least I have Jayce, along with my brother and the other guys.

Jayce Cardea is eighteen and has taken over Head of the Family from his father, John Cardea. But most importantly, he is the one that I love.

Jayce and my brother Aaron are best friends along with Victor's son Nick.

Ben, Jayce's younger brother and their cousin Gage are best friends also.

All the guys along with Nick are really close.

I love all of them but Jayce is different.

I fell in love with Jayce when I was ten years old.

I walked up to him and told him I was going to marry him.

He just looked at me smiling and told me, "Angel, I know you are."

That day was when he truly won me over and we have been together ever since.

In two weeks, I turn sixteen and Jayce and I are getting married.

I know it sounds strange to be getting married at sixteen but since I am the *Principessa* (Princess) – that is what's happening.

In the Mafia Clan the children graduate high school usually at seventeen – the boys take over for their fathers as Head of the Family on their eighteenth birthday.

My best friend Lily and I are the exception.

No, nobody bent any rules for me or her – I earned my diploma as did Lily. We are both really smart, not to brag, it is how we became best friends. We always stuck together since we were always younger than everyone else in our classes.

I learned a lot from the guys, since I was always with them and Lily was always with me. My brother and Jayce sometimes helped me with my homework, but mostly I did it all on my own.

Most girls get married when they are seventeen or eighteen, but with Jayce already Head of the Family – we wanted to go ahead and get married.

Aaron and Alyssa are engaged to be married, so all four of us are having a double wedding.

With Jayce and my brother being best friends – they had decided when they were younger they were going to get married on the same day.

Speaking of Aaron, where is he?

I turn to leave my room and just as I walk by Aaron's room, I noticed his light was on.

Opening the door the person I see is not my brother at all.

"What are you doing in Aaron's room...are you...are you really trying to break in my brother's safe?"

I asked Troy stunned that he was even in here.

Waiting for an explanation, I watched Troy as he shifted back and forth before answering me.

"No ...um...Aaron asked me to get something for him...but the code he gave me is not working...can you try your code...I need to get the vendor list and call him back right away," stuttered out Troy as he looked everywhere but at me.

I had a feeling something wasn't right and there was no way I was letting him in Aaron's safe.

"I can try...but he said something about changing the code yesterday. If he already reset it...my code might not work..."

I began lying making up the story as I looked over at him.

I am very good at lying.

Only a few of the members of my mafia family clan can tell when I am. They should after all, since they are the ones that taught me to lie so well.

My parents always said lying should come easy for me. I should be able to think of a believable lie in under a minute. They have told me it could be the difference between life and death.

Walking over to the safe–I tried entering a wrong code knowing it would not work.

"Sorry...looks like he changed the code after all. You want me to call him and get the code for you?"

I asked him, knowing he did not want me to call my brother.

"No...no that's alright. I'll just ask your dad for the information...I am sure he has a copy of the vendors list...I don't want to bother Aaron...he and the others are at Sea Court Manor."

Troy replied hastily stumbling to get the words out...but what he said...completely threw me off guard.

"What are you talking about...? I thought the meeting wasn't until tomorrow...when did he leave and when is he coming back?"

I demanded completely forgetting that Troy was trying to get inside Aaron's safe.

Troy knew he had distracted me from the fact he was in my brother's room...under questionable reasons.

"He left about two hours ago...and he said he wouldn't be back until around five or six tonight...he said something came up and they had to meet today."

Troy replied before turning and quickly leaving me standing in the middle of Aaron's room confused.

I didn't even realize Troy had left...

I wondered what was so important that Aaron left without leaving me a note.

Looking at the clock on the wall read 7:30...that meant he left at 5:30 this morning!

What would be the reason he would leave at that time of day? I know he didn't want to wake me but I have a feeling something is not right.

Maybe mom knows what is going on since Aaron probably told her before he left.

Leaving Aaron's room I turn and walk down the hall toward the kitchen.

I love the walls on the inside of our house. The logs have such interesting shapes embedded inside the wood. My parents carefully chose each log that made up our home, Haven Manor.

I find mom in the kitchen baking her chocolate-hazelnut biscotti and butter cookies. She loves to bake and has a little café in town.

She bakes all kinds of cookies, cannoli and pastries here at home for the café. Dad told her he would build her whatever kitchen she wanted in the café, but she would rather bake here at home.

"Good morning, mom. Do you know what is going on with Aaron? He left this morning without telling me bye."

I asked her still trying to figure out why the meeting had been changed.

Turning around from the stove; my mom smiles at me before she starts laughing.

"He didn't want to wake you Princess. Jayce called him about five this morning and he left thirty minutes later. I am not sure what is going on but he told me it was nothing to worry about. He said they just needed to take care of a few things. Try not to worry honey. I am sure everything is fine."

"Well ok…if you are sure. Can I borrow your car or…maybe drive my car instead?"

I asked mom knowing Aaron probably hid the key along with the car, since I had no idea where either was.

I figured she might know where it was and I hoped she would say yes; since Aaron was not here to give it to me this morning.

"No, not until your brother gets back. Where are you going?"

"Lily called me and she is trying to finish packing since Larson is coming over in an hour. They are going to Angel Crest Estate since Uncle Stefano wants Larson to pick up Carlos early. Then they are going to head on to Paradise Falls and we are meeting up with them tomorrow…I think. I guess Jayce is coming back with Aaron later since he is supposed to ride with me in my car. I am not sure why Uncle Stefano wanted Larson to go pick up Carlos so early. You and dad are still planning on leaving with us tomorrow…right," I asked wondering if she knew if something had changed.

"That is still the plan as far as I know. Your dad left shortly after your brother to go to work but he didn't tell me anything different. I don't know why Stefano wanted Carlos picked up so early unless there was a change of plans. I will call Carmin while you are at Lily's and try to find out what is going on. Just take my car. How long will you be gone?"

Mom asked me before turning back around to the stove to check the cookies in the oven.

"Not long...Lily just needs my help finishing packing. I don't know how much help I will be. Alyssa is always better at putting outfits together than us."

I told her as I grabbed a drink from the fridge and picked up one of the butter cookies mom just baked...trying to grab it without her seeing me.

"I am sure you will do just fine Arabella. Just promise to be careful driving and try not to speed too much."

Mom told me looking over her shoulder eyeing me as I grabbed another cookie.

"I will mom. Oh...I wanted to ask you. Did you know that Troy was in Aaron's room trying to open his safe," I asked her as she lifted another pan of cookies sliding them in the oven.

"No...wait...what are you talking about," asked Mom closing the oven and turning from the stove to walk over to me, looking as confused as I felt.

"When I came out of my room earlier the lights were on in Aaron's room so I went in there. Troy was in Aaron's room at the safe trying to open it. I asked him what he was doing and he told me that Aaron had asked him to get the vendor list. He said the code that Aaron gave him wouldn't work and asked if I would try mine. Something didn't seem right so I didn't open it for him."

Mom looked at me in surprise at what I had told her; usually nobody is allowed in our bedrooms but family.

I was beginning to think mom didn't even know Troy was in the house.

This is not good, not at all!!

"Well I am glad you didn't open it. Just make sure to tell your brother what happened as soon as he gets home," mom told me as the worry lines around her eyes began to show.

I didn't even ask if she knew Troy was in the house since I could tell she clearly didn't know.

Hugging mom goodbye I grabbed her car keys and headed out the door.

I figured mom would tell dad about Troy when she called him. And knowing mom, she called dad time as I left the house.

The thing with Troy was on my mind the entire drive to Lily's house.

I couldn't figure out what he was up to.

How did he even get in the house…unseen?

Not knowing was starting to make me paranoid.

Lily opened the door to the house as I drove in the drive and was walking toward me, before I could even climb out of the car.

"Hey Arabella, thanks so much for coming over to help me pack. What's going on? You have that funny look on your face again."

Lily demanded looking at me waiting for me to explain...as she stood there with her hand on her hip.

I let out a huge sigh trying to find a way to tell her without scaring her. I knew there was no way to keep it a secret since Lily could always tell when something was wrong.

Looking at my best friend I tried to think of a way to tell her what I had seen on the way over.

I didn't want to scare her...since I was a little scared myself.

"I am seriously paranoid right now. I saw something...I don't think I was supposed to see on the way here. Lily I think something really bad is going on."

I blurted out all in one breath as I watched Lily's eyes widen.

Lily grabbed my hand and started pulling me behind her as she rushed inside the house. I almost fell as she pulled me...running up the stairs to her room.

After we sat down on her bed I told her everything that had happened that day–from Aaron leaving to me finding Troy in my brother's room. By the time I got to the phone call earlier this morning from Jayce...I was having trouble breathing.

"Deep slow breaths, Arabella. You are scaring me and I need you to calm down. Try to slow down your breathing," Lily told me as she held my hand trying to calm both of us.

Finally when I could breathe normal I looked at Lily and told her the rest.

"Lily I saw something...when I was on the way over here. Troy was talking to two men that I have never seen before. One had this weird looking scar...all the way down the left side of his face. It is not like a normal scar...it has this strange odd shape. It kind of looked like...a knife...or feather of some kind."

Lily's eyes grew wide as she grabbed my arm asking, "You don't think he is White Feather, do you?"

I could see the fear in her eyes as she sat beside me gripping my arm.

I had thought the man I saw was White Feather but I didn't want to scare Lily any more than she already was.

"I don't know that it is for sure Lily so try not to worry. Well...you are all packed so where is Larson?"

I asked her trying to get her mind off what I had told her.

Lily just looked at me with fear shining in her eyes.

I could see the wheels turning as she tried to grasp what I had told her.

"Maybe...you should just go with us Arabella. Don't you think we should tell Larson when he gets here? Are you going to call Jayce and your brother...to tell them about Troy and the men," Lily demanded as she tried to piece together a way out of this.

Lily is always trying to solve problems.

I love her for it–but sometimes pulling the trigger is the only way to solve some problems.

But I love her for trying to always find a rainbow–when the thunder clouds are pouring.

I wasn't sure if calling my brother and Jayce was the best idea right now.

I had no idea what they would do…especially since I truly thought the man I saw was White Feather.

I stood up as Lily grabbed her suitcase heading to the stairs.

"I don't know. I don't want to be wrong…and cause a big thing. And you know it would be a big thing. If any of them thought I was in danger…the entire Mafia Clan would come to Haven Falls! You know its true Lily. Besides, I am leaving tomorrow to go to Paradise Falls and Jayce and Aaron are coming home tonight. I think maybe we should keep quiet for now. I see anything else…I promise I will call them."

"Just promise to be careful! Call them right away if anything else happens," Lily insisted as she picked up her bag and we headed toward the door.

"I promise I will be very careful–I will call if I see them again," I told her.

Lily seemed satisfied with my answer as I breathed a sigh of relief.

Lily may be sunshine and rainbows–but I knew she also saw the storms raging.

We headed downstairs just as Larson pulled up in the driveway.

I opened the front door and Lily carried the suitcase over to his truck.

"Hey babe...you ready to go," he asked Lily smiling at both of us as he reached for Lily's suitcase.

Lily nodded her head yes to him–while she kept looking over at me. Larson put her suitcase in the backseat of his truck before turning around to look between me and Lily.

He never asked but he knew something was wrong.

"Did you see Aaron before he left this morning," Larson asked laughing at the thought of my brother waking me up.

"No...he didn't even leave me a note to tell me he was leaving. Mom said Jayce called him at five o'clock this morning and he left thirty minutes later. He told her it was nothing to worry about. Do you know what's going on?"

I asked hoping he had more answers than I did since I knew he had talked to Aaron this morning.

"Arabella...I really don't know what is going on. Aaron called me at six o'clock this morning-asked me if Lily and I would pick up Carlos. He wanted us to pick him up and then meet you all at Paradise Falls tonight. Aaron told me he was bringing Jayce back later today...then all of you were leaving to go back to Paradise Falls tonight. I know Aaron picked up Alyssa to go on with him. He said your father was staying in Haven Falls until he and Jayce got back. All he told me was the meeting had been changed to today. He said it was fine that your dad and I weren't there...that Stefano needed me to go get Carlos right away."

Larson replied as he watched me closely before reaching out to put his hand on my arm, steading me as I began to sway.

Looking up at Larson–I had no clue what to say. As I tried to steady my breathing–so many different scenarios were running through my head...I couldn't think straight.

What had happened to make my dad stay here...miss a meeting? He has never missed a meeting before! They always wait until they are all together to meet so that everyone is included.

That meant I was right, something is very wrong...

Calling my brother or Jayce right now seemed like a good idea–except for the town exploding!

It would be better to go by the station and talk the Dad. I could tell him what I saw and he would know what to do. Plus as a bonus...he couldn't get too mad since I will be right in front of him. I think...

Looking up at Larson I knew I should tell him what I saw earlier, so I did.

When I was finished I asked him, "Can you think of a good way for me to tell Aaron and Jayce...without the whole town exploding?"

Larson busted out laughing before answering me.

"I have no clue. But you have them both wrapped around your finger, so just tell them to chill the hell out."

I shook my head at him as he smiled down at me. Larson was really something sometimes–but right now I was too worried and scared to be mad at him.

I hugged Lily goodbye...I watched as they drove off down the street until I could no longer see the truck before turning back to the car.

I got in mom's car and headed toward the station to see dad. With any luck mom had already called him and told him about Troy.

I had really picked a great day to leave home without my guns!! Never again...besides after my brother and the other guys find out I didn't bring a gun-I wouldn't be surprised if they said I am not allowed to go anywhere unarmed again!!!

My luck they will make it a Clan Rule:

Arabella must be armed at all times-she is not allowed to leave the house without a loaded gun.

But at least that will keep things like this from not happening...again!!

Chapter 2

Still trying to find the nerve to call Jayce and my brother...

I drove toward the station wondering if I should go ahead and call someone and tell them what I had seen on the way to Lily's.

Just as I went around the curve I saw the car again.

Slowing down I pulled mom's car behind the trees, so not to be seen.

I watched as four men started up toward the Haven Sheriff Station.

Just before they could cross the street I saw my dad coming out of the station with his gun in his hand. I watched as my dad walked toward the men.

The man I saw earlier with the scar raised his gun and shot dad....

He didn't even have time to raise his gun.

I saw the blood pouring down his shirt as dad's body fell to the ground.

I had never seen someone best my dad; he is well feared across Italy as well as America ...and it would take someone crazy in my opinion–to even point a gun at him!

I reached down for my phone...as I watched my father's body fall to the ground. My hands were shaking as I dialed Jayce.

The phone only rang once before Jayce answered.

"Angel, is everything ok?"

"No...something really bad has happened! Where's Aaron?"

I yelled as I tried to piece together what to do.

"He is right here...baby, what's going on? Hold on, Angel. Ok...now you are on speaker," Jayce told me just before I heard Aaron's voice came over the line.

"Princess...what's wrong? Talk to me," my brother said calmly trying to sooth me.

I tried to calm down but my hands were shaking.

I was so pissed that I had left my guns at home.

I never thought I would need them today.

I was going to see my best friend! Why would I even think to bring a gun?

I told them both...as I watched the men talking as they looked down at my father's body, "Aaron, Jayce...I am in mom's car here at the curve down from dad's work. Four men got out of a black SUV and walked up to the station and one of them shot dad. Aaron, dad was armed and he didn't even have time to raise his gun to shoot before that guy shot him. Listen to me...I am unarmed and alone so I need one of you to tell me what to do right now!"

Aaron's calm voice came clearly through the pink ear buds in my ear – they had been a gift from Ben and Gage last Christmas.

Aaron told me to turn the car around and started giving me directions. He had me make several turns and before long I could see Haven Manor up ahead.

"Arabella...listen you need to get out of the car and quietly walk up to the door on the right side of the garage," Aaron told me as I drove up to Haven Manor.

I asked him what he wanted me to do with mom's car...as I drove up behind Haven Manor along the backside of the property.

"Park it where it is hidden...over in the bushes."

Aaron answered as I pulled the car behind a row of trees and shrubbery.

I pulled the left ear bud out of my ear...so I could hear around me and left the right one in for the phone.

I took a look around and parked the car.

I quietly closed the door behind me and started walking slowly toward the garage.

Before I had reached the end of the tree line where I would no longer be hidden, Jayce's loud voice filled my ear.

"Angel, stop...stay where you are! Don't move someone is walking in your direction."

"How do you know that?"

I whispered never doubting what he said as I stayed perfectly still.

"Aaron and I are watching you and the house on the monitors. Just stay where you are for a minute."

I wasn't sure who they were–but if they were in the house then it might be best I don't go in.

"Are they inside the house," I asked them as I looked around the tree toward Haven Manor.

It took a second before Jayce answered, "Yes Angel...there are two men inside."

Well that was just perfect!

These two were sending me into a house with bad guys and no gun.

This made no sense...

"Are you sure...this is the smartest idea? You want to send me into the house with armed men...and I don't even have a gun. Are you both crazy?"

I could hear several voices talking over one another thru the ear bud in my ear–but I couldn't make out everything they said or even who said it.

I heard Uncle Vic and John saying something about my mom. But before I could ask, Aaron started talking as he tried to convince me to go in the house.

"Arabella…you know I won't let anything happen to you. I need you to get into the house…in order for me to get you out of Haven Falls. There are guns in the house, and I promise as soon as you get inside you can grab one. It will be ok Princess…I promise. Just listen and do what we tell you and you will be here with us soon. Ok?"

I was not happy about this at all but I trust my brother.

There were guns in the house and I needed a gun, like right now!

The only problem was I had to get inside without any of these guys seeing me.

"Ok, just tell me what to do," I replied as I took a deep breath and listened.

It was easy to put my faith in my brother and Jayce. I could always count on them to keep me safe.

Jayce told me when it was clear and I quietly ran up to the door.

Aaron gave me the code to unlock the door. I opened the door and slipped inside the garage.

My brother talked me through two doors stopping to grab a gun before I came into an open one car garage.

"Aaron…is that my car?"

I asked almost in a state of shock as I heard my brother and Jayce laughing over the phone–both of them told me this was my car as I stood there looking it over.

Before me stood a shiny black SUV with pink trim, including completely bulletproof body, glass, and four tires.

To say no one could get to me while I was inside was an understatement...

But I knew there was no way they would let me have something that didn't protect me.

I really didn't care what kind of car they gave me. I had only told them it had to be black and pink, with an awesome sound system–and of course all the girl stuff inside.

I walked up to open the doors only to find them locked...so I asked Aaron where the key was.

"The key is inside my room. Let's go. We have to get you in the house. Arabella, the room you are in now is secure; as well as the way you are going to your room. Take the black door on your right, and follow the tunnel until you see a black and pink door."

I walked to the door and open it and walked around into the passageway. The black and pink door was just ahead and to the left.

I opened the door and was surprised to find I had walked right into my bedroom.

Mom and Dad always said that my bedroom, The Principessa Chamber, as they called it–was the most secure room in the entire house.

They always said my room held precious treasures that could never be replaced.

Now I'm beginning to see exactly what they meant–since I just came thru a freaking secret door I never knew was there!

Aaron told me to grab my bags that were already packed for the trip to Paradise Falls tomorrow.

He had me grab a few other things from secret doors he had me open throughout my room. Every time I asked him about them...he said he would tell me later.

There was an old mahogany box that my brother had me get that was hidden behind a secret panel...within the frame under my bed. I have been sleeping in this bed for as long as I can remember- and I certainly didn't know about any secret panels!!

So I ask Aaron what it was and who had put it inside my bed.

"Dad and Victor had your bed made...so I guess one of them. As to what it is...I have no clue. Stefano is talking to Victor now and Victor said to get the box inside your bed. I really don't know anything else Princess. Stefano is not talking."

Aaron said sounding as confused as I felt!

After I had grabbed everything and placed it on the other side of the door I came through...Aaron told me where my car key was.

"Now listen...the key is in my room in my right drawer. There is a hidden door behind the back of the mirror in your bathroom. Now my room is not secure...so as soon as I say go, you have to grab the key and get back in your bathroom. As soon as you close the mirror back the security lock engages again."

Aaron told me as I walked across my bedroom to the bathroom door on the left side of the room.

I took a deep breath and told them to tell me when to go.

As soon as the coast was clear, Aaron had me open the mirror.

I ran to the dresser and open the drawer; there was a black box tied with pink ribbon inside so I grabbed it.

As soon as I was back in my bathroom and the mirror lock engaged…

I heard footsteps coming down the hall.

Jayce told me when to move and I quietly walked back in my room.

I started heading back the way I came but before I made it a few feet…I turned back toward my bedroom door.

Before I could take a step I heard Aaron's panic voice loudly in my ear.

"Don't even think about it Arabella. You go straight to the car, right now!"

I turned and left my bedroom going in the direction of the garage–like my brother told me. As soon as I was through the passageway and back in the garage with all the bags, I opened the box for the key.

There was a note in the box with the car key but I would have to read it later.

I unlocked the car and loaded the bags in the back seat.

"Aaron…where is mom? Can I go get mom now?"

I pleaded with my brother not wanting to leave my mom behind.

His voice sounded harsh when he answered me.

"No Arabella, you have to go now! Get in the car."

I knew I had no choice since the men here would figure out I was here and come for me.

Aaron told me how to turn on the car security systems and then how to open the hidden wall in the garage.

The amount of hidden passage ways and walls in my house that I knew nothing of…was to say the least, shocking!

As soon as the wall opened I drove thru to find yet another tunnel.

As I started driving the wall behind me closed taking all the light. Before I could ask Aaron how to turn on the headlights; the lights before me begin to light up all the way down.

I followed along turning only twice when Aaron said right and then a left turn. I told Aaron and Jayce about what had happened earlier that day with Troy and the men.

Of course the only saving grace was I was already on the way to them, the town was spared for now at least.

Only I didn't know what had happened to the town or anyone there. I knew my dad and probably my mom were both dead.

What about everyone else?

Before I could ask either of them these questions out loud…

I heard Jayce and Aaron both growl angrily.

When I asked what was going on…my brother told me White Feather had just walked into our house. I had to ask them what was happening–since I didn't know how to make the on-board security monitoring system in the car work.

And there was no way I was going to stop and try to turn it on!

Jayce and Aaron told me that White Feather was trying to get into my bedroom and that he was looking for me.

"What do you mean he is looking for me Jayce? What does he want with me? How much longer until I get out of here? I don't want him to find me guys!"

I rambled on as I began to panic at the thought of White Feather so close.

Jayce's calm voice filled my ears, "Angel, he is not going to get you, I promise. You will be in my arms in about thirty minutes. Don't worry, you are safe now."

Puzzled as to what he could possibly be thinking since there was no way my car could fly…maybe he didn't mean that or I heard it wrong.

"What do you mean thirty minutes? You are over an hour away! I can't fly in this car unless there is something you forgot to tell me."

I was beginning to think my brother and Jayce were crazy for sure.

I mean look at the facts:

They send me unarmed into a house with bad guys and now seem to think I can make a little over an hour trip, in thirty minutes.

"The tunnels you are in are a straight shot either way between all the towns. They make for a quicker escape to get from Haven Falls to any of the other towns. Arabella…I know how you drive and I am sure you are driving at least seventy right now," Aaron told me as he explained how to get from one town to another, thru the tunnels.

It made sense–our father and the elders were a paranoid bunch. For them to have built secret grottos underground between the towns as means of an escape, sounded just like them.

It is no crazier than the fact they have buried gas lines surrounding the houses and shops in each of the four towns.

At least when the elders built all of the houses for the family; they built them twenty miles or more from the center of each of the four individual towns, so they wouldn't blow-up too!

"Aaron…who all knows about these tunnels," I asked thinking about Troy.

If he could get into Aaron's bedroom without mom even seeing him, who knows what he knows about.

"Don't worry Princess only the head of each family and of course our fathers, since they built them," Aaron replied.

It made sense that no one else knew…hell I was the Princess and I didn't even know about them!

I drove as fast as safely possible, wanting to get to Jayce and Aaron. The only thing keeping me somewhat sane was thinking that Lily should be ok.

"Hey have you heard from Larson? Are he and Lily ok?"

Jayce answered me right away, "We just talked to Larson and he and Lily are fine they made it to Carlos. They are on the way to Paradise Falls right now. Lily was not happy that Larson would not let her call you…she wanted to turn around and go get you. I promised her you were fine and that I would have you call her as soon as you get here. Stefano had to talk to her, to promise her that you were ok before she would calm down."

I smiled at the thought of my best friend; I know she is giving Larson and the others a hard time.

She is a little scary when she is mad–but you would never know she is such a firecracker, as tiny as she is.

But then again, so am I with the exception I can shoot a gun.

And of course there is Lily's sunshine optimism which has been my saving grace a few times over the years.

Lily and I both are very tiny and dainty looking–where her hair is black mine is golden blond. My hair is long with ringlets of curls that I can never get to straighten–Lily is straight and never holds a curl, no matter what we do.

We like to say we are each other's yin and yang. But as different as our hair is everything else is pretty much the same. We both have blue eyes; but mine tend to change from dark blue like a stormy sky to light blue like the ocean, depending on my moods.

We wear the same size in clothes and are forever trading them back and forth; to the point it drove our moms crazy.

Thinking about my parents I realized Lily's parents might be dead too.

Before I could stop it tears started slowing falling down my cheek.

I sniffled as I tried to stop the flow of water continuing to pour from my eyes. I wiped my face with my hands and took in a deep breath.

I had to get it together; I was driving and now was not the time to have a breakdown.

"Baby, are you crying?" Jayce asked me softly.

"Yeah...but I'm ok now so how much further," I told Jayce as I wiped my face again.

All I had to do was keep on driving until I got to Jayce and my brother. I couldn't fall apart right now I had to get out of Haven Falls before White Feather found me.

"Arabella, can you see the light at the end of the tunnel ahead yet?"

I could see daylight shining up ahead of me at the opening in the tunnel.

"Yes...I see it. Where does it come out to?"

I asked hoping it came out to where ever he was.

I was sure I had been driving at least twenty minutes so that had to be Paradise Falls up ahead.

"I'm at the end Angel. I am right here waiting for you."

Chapter 3

I looked checking the seat beside me to make sure both my pistols where there within reach. They were a thing of beauty my guns, 9 mm solid black with pink trim and they shot like a dream.

They were both given to me for my 15th birthday from Jayce.

He even had angel wings engraved in the handles.

I could hit a target dead on no matter where I aimed.

After all I had learned everything I know from the best. All of the original Clan members; along with the best hit-man in Italy had taught me how to shoot.

Every one of them said as the only girl, I had to be able to shoot as well but better than the boys.

Now don't get me wrong they all can shoot; Jayce, Aaron and Nick are the best out of all the boys.

I of course am right there with them!

When I was ten years old my parents took me and Aaron to Italy to see Victor.

Of course Jayce went with Aaron; since both wanted to see Nick.

Victor, or Uncle Vic to me, said if I wanted to learn some tricks shooting my gun that I should get Buono to teach me.

So I went after Buono with my shiny pink gun in my hands.

I found him out in the vineyards and walked over to ask him to teach me a few tricks. Nick and the guys were out playing by the vineyards and looked over where I stood with Buono.

"Excuse me sir…Uncle Vic said you might be able to show me some of your shooting tricks," I politely asked, as I had been taught manners were very important for a princess.

Hearing my voice, Buono turned to look down at me.

"A little girl like you shouldn't play with guns that you don't know how to shoot. You should take your toy gun and go play somewhere else," he told me while laughing as he looked down at me.

I of course, knew he was not using nice manners and he needed to be punished.

Dad always said everyone should treat me with respect and that I should demand to be treated like a lady.

Well seeing as how I was only ten and the guy before me was easily three times my size; I was left with only one option.

Before he could turn back around I raised my gun and shot him in the right arm–since it was his shooting arm.

Shooting him in the left arm was not really a punishment and he had been very rude to me.

It wasn't bad–just a nick the bullet went thru and thru the outside of his right upper arm.

Seeing what I had done Nick and the other began running over to me.

Later I would find out everyone including my father was coming to save me …

Or so they thought.

You see no one shoots Buono Ferrero and lives. He is notorious and is Victor's right hand man, not to mention he is the Mafia's most feared hit-man.

But Buono…he just looks down at me and burst out laughing.

"Well little lady would you please tell me why you shot me?"

I explained that he had used bad manners and needed to be taught a lesson.

When he asked what he should do about the two bleeding holes in his arm, I replied my pink Band-Aids would fix him right up.

So, off I went to help him patch up his arm with my pink and black stripe Band-Aids.

Before we could walk back to the villa, Jayce had ran over and told Buono he would kill him if he tried to hurt me.

Seeing Jayce along with my brother and Nick – now all holding guns pointed at him…

Buono only nodded his head and told him he meant me no harm.

After telling Jayce I was going to marry him…

Buono and I went to go patch up his arm.

We all became great friends after that day. Although, Uncle Vic swears Buono fell in love with me on the spot after I shot him.

He taught me different tricks shooting my gun and then joined Uncle Vic and me for a tea party that afternoon.

"I'm almost to the end of the tunnel Jayce. I can see the sunlight shining though the opening."

I told him as the end of the tunnel came closer.

Finally I drove out of the tunnels and the road began to climb upwards.

I could see Jayce and Aaron at the top of the hill and began to drive faster.

When I was close enough to Aaron's truck I stopped the car. Before I could get the car in park the driver's door flew open as Jayce reached for me. I held onto Jayce as he pulled out of the car and into his arms.

Aaron was beside Jayce, so he reached over hugging me too; so that I was now in the middle of my two favorite guys. For the first time since all this began I finally felt safe.

I didn't want them to know just how scared I really was...but I was mad too. Really mad, mad at myself for leaving my gun home this morning and mad at White Feather for killing my dad. I was sure it was him and that scared me even more.

He shot my dad before he even had a chance to shoot back.

How did White Feather even find us and why now after all these years?

But what truly scared me more than anything...

Was the fact that I had no idea what would happen now.

Uncle Vic is on his way here and I know something really bad is about to happen. I just wonder what will be left standing when the dust settles.

"Angel...are you ok...are you hurt baby?"

Jayce asked as he looked me over from head to toe checking for injuries.

I told them both I was fine and asked what was happening back at Haven Falls. Neither would answer my questions–just told me we had to get going.

Aaron got in his truck and Jayce and I took my car.

Jayce began driving with my brother following close behind.

"Are you sure you are ok baby?"

Jayce asked as he held my hand tightly in his.

I knew my dad was dead, I saw White Feather kill him but what about my mom. I looked up at him and nodded my head before I started talking.

"Yes I'm ok. Jayce is my mom ok? What happened after I left Haven? What is happening at Haven Manor with my mom, tell me please?"

He only squeezed my hand as he looked over at me before turning to look out the window as he drove.

"Wait until we get to Sea Court Manor Angel. Everyone is waiting on you."

"Who is everyone? Jayce why was the meeting changed? Why didn't my dad go? Please tell me what is going on," I pleaded.

I knew there was something they were not telling me.

Why would my dad miss a meeting?

It's not like they thought White Feather was in Haven Falls or they all would have been there.

Right?

"Everyone is at Sea Court Manor with the exception of Rocco, your father and Victor. Stefano called Victor right after you called me…he is on his way now with Nick and Buono," said Jayce as he drove looking from me to the road.

"Dad and Uncle Benito had to almost restrain Stefano and Costa when they found out you were in Haven alone. They never thought you would be in danger or that you would be alone with none of us there. I have never heard so many Italian curse words in all my life said in the same conversation as Stefano, Costa and Victor were having. As soon as dad heard about Carmin…he called Rocco and told him to come home. Dad is ready to kill someone baby. Your dad was his best friend and my mom is worst. She told me not to come back without you…or I would be very sorry. Of course I never would!"

Jayce took a breath almost like whatever he was about to say was painful.

"Angel I don't think I have ever been so scared. Knowing you were alone...unarmed and were in danger and I couldn't get to you almost killed me. I told Aaron that I would kill everyone...and anyone who got in my way to get to you," Jayce told me as he squeezed my hand tightly.

Listening to Jayce broke my heart because I would be the same way if it was him.

"Jayce...I think Troy was the one who let White Feather into town. I just can't figure out why he was in Aaron's room trying to get in the safe. He never keeps anything really worth stealing in there anyway. Apparently everything that is worth stealing was hidden in my bedroom...in secret panels and doors that I knew nothing about!"

I told him as I thought about how I could have missed all the hidden panels and doors in my own bedroom.

"We know...we believe he is also working with Oscar. We were watching the feed from the town. Oscar seemed really friendly with two of the men you saw. Everyone is as you described...except we can't find the man with the scar. We think you're right and he is White Feather. He was wearing a feather mask so we never got to see his face. We believe that Troy told him about you...but we are not sure of what. But we will find out Angel and then I will kill them all. None of them will get to you," Jayce swore to me as he looked over at me.

I could see in his eyes. No one would be left alive if they came in his path.

I knew he meant it. I felt kind sorry for anyone who tried to hurt me...

But then I remembered who was after me and the feeling passed as quickly as it came.

Jayce drove us up in front of his father's house. We got out and started walking up toward the door. Before we made it past the car – the door flew open and Gage and Ben came running out.

Ben got to me first...grabbing me in a hug only to be pulled away by Gage. Ben looked at his brother pouting before he began demanding that Gage let me go.

> "Jayce...tell Gage to give her back to me. He took her from me instead of waiting his turn. Princess would say that's not nice manners. I want to hug my soon to be sister-in-law..."

Ben whined to his brother all the while laughing as he gave Gage the evil eye.

Aaron started laughing, telling them both I wasn't going anywhere they needed to take turns.

After they both calmed down we turned to all walk in the house together.

Jayce and Ben are brothers...

They look alike but are two years apart. Both stand tall at around six feet with blond hair and dark blue eyes; but Jayce is twice the size of Ben with muscles.

My brother is built like Jayce...

They are both the same size and height. Where my hair is golden blond; Aaron has more brown in his blond and his eyes are a dark deep green.

Gage and Ben are built the same; sharing the same color blond hair and blue eyes. You would think that Gage and Ben were brothers rather than cousins...

They have been close since the day they were born.

Nick is the only one of us without blond hair. His is hair is black as night and his eyes are a bright green. Nick is the same size as Jayce and my brother.

The three of them use to call themselves the Three Mafia Brothers when they were little.

I was glad Nick was coming; I miss him terribly. I know I am going to see him when we go to Italy in a month but we don't get to see him often enough.

The reason for this visit wasn't far from my mind...

I wondered what would happen when Victor arrived.

Living in this family, you learn to deal with death and killing from a young age.

We understand it – we just react differently than most people.

"So Peanut...are you really ok?" Gage asked me.

Gage is the only person that calls me peanut.

Gage started calling me peanut when he was six years old. Our parents ask him why he was calling me peanut–he told them he loved peanut butter more than anything else in the world and me too, so he was nicknaming me Peanut.

He outgrew his love for peanut butter around the age of nine...but the name stayed.

"I'm ok," I told him as I squeezed his hand as we walked into the house.

Everyone turned as we walked in the room...

Jayce's mom Marie was the first one to reach me...pushing everyone out of her way. She hugged me, fussing over me; checking me from head to toe, just like her sons had done.

Of course Uncle Stefano and Costa were beside themselves pacing back and forth grumbling.

I could see what Jayce meant about them being mad.

I could hear Uncle Victor over the speaker phone asking me if I had gotten the box that was inside the hidden door under my bed.

I told him that it was in the backseat of my car.

Uncle Benny took off outside to get the box as soon as I told Victor and they others where it was. He brought it inside and then disappeared for a minute before coming back into the room empty handed.

No one said a word about the box and I could tell it wasn't the best time to ask.

But I knew whatever it was it had to be important.

Apparently so important...it needed to be hidden!

Uncle Stefano wanted to know everything that had happened. So Uncle John and Benny had me sit down on the couch and go over everything that had happened since I woke up this morning.

Yes, I call all the original mafia clan members Uncle...just one of the perks of being me.

Uncle John pulled me to the side after I had finished telling them what had happened.

> "*Tesoro* (sweetheart), I am truly sorry about your parents but the people responsible will pay, you have my word. Your father was my best friend and I will avenge his and your mother's death."

Tears began to fall down my face as I looked up at him.

I knew they were both dead...

I could see it in their faces when I walked in earlier.

> "Uncle John when are you all going to Haven Falls? I need to go back. I have to see my mom and dad...please."

Stefano was the one who spoke out in response to my question.

> "Arabella, Victor is on his way and he will be here in the morning. We will all leave and go to Haven Falls together. I know Carmin locked down Haven Falls...so we will need you and Aaron to get in. For now you go with Jayce and get some rest *amore* (love)."

Jayce took me by the hand as we turned and headed out of the house. We were followed by Aaron and Alyssa then Ben and Gage.

Just before we got to my car…

My brother walked over and pulled me in his arms so my head was lying against his chest with my ear over his heart. Aaron always gave me the best hugs.

"Princess, Alyssa and I are heading over to our house since I need to make a few calls. Don't forget to call Lily. Now you go on with Jayce and try to rest a little. I will call Jayce later and we will all get together for supper. Ok sweetie?"

All I could do was nod my head yes as I listened to his heart beating in my ears. I always love my big brother's hugs because I always got to hear his heart.

Aaron's heart always beat strong and steady, never faltering no matter what was going on around him.

Most people's heart rate increases when they are scared or excited but not Aaron's. His heart always beat strong and true.

After promising me he would see me later; he turned and walked me over to my car and waited until I got in the front seat before closing the door. He then opened the backdoor and took out the bag with the things I had packed earlier…from the different secret places in my bedroom.

I turned around in my seat and asked him about them; but he told me we would talk about it later. After shutting the door he walked to the front of the car and talking to Jayce a few minutes–before taking the bag and heading to his truck.

Ben and Gage followed Aaron out as they each headed toward their houses.

Jayce and I got in my car and headed in the same direction.

Jayce had built me my dream house Legacy Meadows Estate…that he had promised me when I was five years old.

The inside was made with large red cedar logs, just like our fathers wanted but the outside was limestone, just like our mothers wanted.

The elders may have decided to build the town out of log wood "like in the olden days" as they always say–but their wives insisted the outside of all the buildings had to be limestone and sandstone.

All the houses and shops in the four towns along with the winery buildings were built this way.

I had carefully decorated our home so that it fit us both perfectly.

Aaron had built Story Brooke Manor for him and Alyssa here in Paradise Falls.

Jayce and my brother had decided two years ago that they were going to join Paradise Falls and Haven Falls together when they turned 18 and took over for their fathers.

Jayce had said with us getting married and me heir to Angels Falls and Angels Paradise – by them joining Paradise Falls and Haven Falls all four towns would be together as one.

I knew that the end goal was to join all four towns together to make one united family. I didn't care either way, I was just glad I didn't have to worry about running two towns on my own.

Also, I loved the fact that my brother was going to be closer to me and Jayce.

I could see our house as we came round the curve. This was home, now the only home I had. I just lost my childhood home and I knew we would never live there again.

Now that we were here at Legacy Meadows everything that had happened today began to hit me all at once.

Jayce pulled my car into the garage and parked it in my spot. I got out the car as Jayce pulled my bags from the back seat.

We walked into the house and headed straight to our bedroom.

Jayce put my bags in the closet before walking over and pulling me into his arms. I knew there was no way I could keep it together any longer as I broke down crying, as Jayce held me.

"Angel I fell in love with you the first time I saw you. You were only a few hours old when your dad put you in my arms. You were so small and so perfect. Everyone in that room fell in love with you that day."

Jayce tilted my face up with his hands so he could look in my eyes.

He wiped the tears from my face as he placed a kiss on my forehead.

"Please, don't stop. Jayce tell me the story. I love this story and I love you," I begged him as I looked up at him.

It was true I loved this story...

Jayce and Aaron had told me this story hundreds of times but I never tire of hearing it.

He took me by the hand and led me to our bed. Together we crawled up to the head of the bed and I sat back against the headboard. I waited until Jayce was sitting on the bed to hear the rest of the story.

Just before he sat back he reached over and opened the drawer in the nightstand by our bed and pulled out a box. He sat back and handed me the box to open.

Inside were our wedding rings and my engagement ring.

"I picked it up yesterday; the jeweler just finished your ring. Open it up and tell me what you think," Jayce said as he watched to see my reaction when I saw the ring for the first time.

I opened the box to find the most beautiful rings I had ever seen.

My diamond was a 4 carat princess-cut black diamond engagement ring with pink diamonds surrounding the stone and then running down the band on both sides.

My wedding band had small square black and pink diamonds going all the way around the entire ring. Jayce's ring was made with black diamonds all the way around the band.

They were perfect, since black was Jayce's favorite color and black and pink were mine.

Jayce took my diamond ring out of the box and slipped it on my hand.

"Jayce I love it and it fits perfect! I can't wait to marry you. I don't know what is going to happen now. I know we have our wedding all planned...but my dad is gone Jayce. I don't have anyone to walk me down the aisle. Mom is gone and there is probably no one left in Haven Falls to come. I want to marry you I don't want to wait. What are we going to do?"

I asked thinking about how my parents wouldn't be there to see us get married.

Jayce looked at me as he held my hand his finger running over the diamond on my hand.

"Angel I don't know but we will figure it out. Let me talk to Aaron and we will work something out for the wedding. I am marrying you the day you turn sixteen, one way or another. I promise baby you will be my wife on your birthday. That is the only present you wanted for your birthday and you will have it I promise."

"At least we know your 19th birthday party will be awesome. I miss Nick...I know he is on his way but they won't stay long. I love Italy and I can't wait to go back. Uncle Vic was having a ball planning the party when I talked to him last week. He is so excited about us going to Italy and staying for the month. You know I think it is so cool that you, Nick and my brother were born so close together. Especially since there is always three different types of birthday cakes for me to eat! I told Uncle Vic to get you a chocolate cake with the sweet cherries you like," I told him thinking about the upcoming trip.

The birthdays in our family are just a little weird.

My parents along with the others lived in Italy when my brother and the guys were born. My mom Annabel, Jayce's mom Marie and Nick's mom were all pregnant at the same time.

Nick was born first on July 1st, followed by Jayce the next day and finally Aaron was born on July 3rd. They all grew up and lived together...until my father and the other's decided to move to America.

Jayce and Aaron were almost two years old then. I didn't come until a little over a year later.

Marie and Julianna were both pregnant with Ben and Gage when they moved. They were born six months later both on August 2nd ...they were only a few hours apart.

And if that isn't weird enough for you, think about this...

My birthday is on June 18th, Nick on July 1st, Jayce on July 2nd following Aaron on July 3rd.

Then there is Ben and Gage born on the same day, August 3rd. Benito was born on October 11th with Stefano and Costa both being born on October 19th...five hours apart.

But here is where it gets really weird!

Victor was born on November 20th, John the next day and then finally ending with my father born on November 22nd. All three were born a day apart...in the same order as their sons.

Nick, Jayce and Aaron all swear their sons will all be born the same year in July on the same day...their birthdays. I think they are crazy because this is something that has been going on since they were ten!

Apparently, when they were playing together that summer Nick was telling them about what had happened back home in Italy. Some of the vineyard workers were betting money on when two of the workers wife's babies would be born.

Since they didn't have any money to bet they thought of something else. The three of them have never told anyone what the winner of the bet gets–they only say it's a blood-secret between Three Mafia Brothers.

I think every one of them is crazy and Ben and Gage agree with me.

They had decided they were all having their sons born on the same day, so they could grow up together...like them.

They each bet that all the boys would be born on one of the guys' birthday.

So that meant that all three boys would be born the same year on July 1st, 2nd or 3rd.

Which day depended on which of the three you asked...and all three thought they were right.

Jayce has been telling me for as long as I can remember that when we have our son, he will be born on July 2nd along with Nick and Aaron's.

I really have no clue what would happen if we have a little girl instead and she's not born on his birthday!

Chapter 4

Jayce takes the ring box, minus the diamond that is on my finger and puts it back in the drawer by the bed.

He sits back and looks over at me.

"Do you want to lie down and try to sleep awhile?"

"No, I can't sleep. Will you tell me the rest of the story," I asked leaning back against the bed.

He began telling me the story I had heard hundreds of times over the years but it was still my favorite.

"Angel I fell in love with you the first time I saw you. You were only a few hours old when your dad put you in my arms. You were so small and so perfect. Everyone in that room fell in love with you that day. The day you were born was the one and only time I ever hit Nick. You had just been born – they had cleaned you up and had put you in a little white sundress. Everyone in the waiting room was anxiously waiting to meet the first baby girl born in our families. Aaron, Nick and I were at the door so we could see as soon as your dad came out. Mom and Aunt Julianna were at our house with the babies. Ben and Gage were only ten months old so they were too small to go to the hospital. Victor, Dad and the others were walking back and forth so much they wore a hole in the carpet.

Finally your dad came to get us, he told us we could come in and see you. We all walked into the room and there you were. Your mom had you in her arms wrapped in a pink blanket. The three of us were too short to see you so Aaron told his dad to give you to him. Your dad told us we would have to take turns and since Aaron was the brother he went first. Aaron crawled up into the chair and your dad laid you in his arms. Aaron took one look at you and called you a princess. That is why everyone calls you Princess, Angel. It was my turn next so I crawled up into the chair and your dad gave you to me. I looked down at you and called you an angel. I told everyone in the room that I was going to marry you. Since that day I have always called you Angel.

Stefano walked over to where I was holding you and looked down at you and said, "She is a Principessa and *un angelo* (an angel), she will be the one that brings this *famiglia insieme come uno solo* (family together as one). Arabella Marcello you will be my sole heir, Angels Falls is yours *amore* (love)."

After Stefano said he was naming you sole heir, Costa named you sole heir of Angels Paradise as well. Nick said my time was up and it was his turn to hold you too. I didn't want to let you go, but my dad said I had to give Nick a turn. After your dad picked you up I walked over to Nick. I looked him in the eyes and told him you were mine and punched him in the nose. He got to hold you but he never tried to take you away from me. I meant you were mine...Angel I don't share."

Jayce took me in his arms and kissed me like I belonged to him and him alone.

I have loved him from the time he tried to rescue me from Buono…after I shot him. He ran right up to Buono and told him he would kill him if he tried to hurt me.

I told him I was going to marry him…he told me that he already knew.

From that moment at 10 years old in Italy I knew I had found my prince.

Daddy always said every princess needs a strong and brave prince. Jayce standing up to Buono who was three times his size; I knew then and there I had found my prince.

Jayce might have known he was going to marry me at three years old but it took until I was ten before I finally agreed.

Jayce had been telling me all my life I was going to marry him.

Once when I was five I was playing with Lily in my bedroom. We were playing house with our dolls but of course each doll had a pink or black gun.

Our idea of playing house was a little different than most girls. Our dolls were super power mafia dolls.

I had my doll in my hand and was telling Lily that I would marry Nick. I was talking about the doll "Sally" was marrying doll "Nick", but of course that is not what Jayce thought!

Jayce and Aaron were walking by my room while we were playing and overheard us talking. Of course, Jayce thinks I mean his friend Nick not "Nick the doll" and comes storming into my room.

Jayce walks right up to me and bends down to look in my eyes.

He calmly says to me, "Angel you can't marry Nick. You are going to marry me and I am going to build you a dream house."

I didn't understand why he is telling me this since I never said I was going to marry Nick.

Lily of course tells Jayce that I wasn't marrying Nick, because Nick is marrying Sally.

This of course causes my brother to fall to the floor laughing before telling Jayce that I was talking about the dolls.

"Ok then…Angel you play with your dolls. Aaron and I will be in his room, so yell if you need anything. I will come back and get you both in an hour and we will all go to Gino's."

He kissed me on the top of my head and he and Aaron went to play.

So marrying Jayce was something I had waited all my life to do.

Aaron met Alyssa when they were sixteen years old. He asked her to marry him on her seventeenth birthday. Aaron got down on one knee with a ring and flowers and asked her to marry him.

I told her I was jealous–Jayce had told me since birth I was going to marry him he never even asked me.

Aaron and Jayce always said they would get married on the same day so that their kids could all grow up together.

I couldn't marry Jayce until I turned sixteen and graduate high school.

Aaron and Alyssa decided to wait until after I was sixteen to get married. I wanted to get married on my birthday, so we are having a double wedding in two weeks.

Oh, thinking of birthday's Lily's birthday is coming up soon. She turns sixteen nine days after me and I have to go get her present.

"Jayce, I need to get a present for Lily's birthday. Do you think you can take me into town? I wanted go by the antique store. They had an antique perfume set I wanted to get her," I asked Jayce thinking about what else to pick up for Lily.

"Of course Angel I will take you. When do you want to go," he asked me lying down across our bed.

"Right now... if that's ok," I told him not wanting to wait.

Jayce got up from the bed pulling me with him and headed toward the door. I told him I was going to freshen up before we left. I followed Jayce to the car after combing my hair and pulling it into a ponytail that I knew would fall out before we got to the car.

Jayce took me into town...

I got the perfume set along with a blue butterfly hair clip for Lily.

Aaron had called Jayce while I was finishing up in the store.

We were now on the way to meet them at Cardea Steakhouse. Gage and Ben were meeting us there along with Larson, Lily and Carlos.

I had called Lily earlier while Jayce was driving us home.

Jayce didn't want to ask me anymore questions knowing I had just told everything, just moments before. He had told me to call Lily and talk to her on the way home.

Lily of course, was not happy Larson wouldn't take her back to Haven Falls to get me.

Larson had called Aaron on their way out of town to tell him what I had told him. I knew when he and Lily left this morning that he would be calling my brother to tell him about Troy and the men.

I didn't blame him for calling Aaron. He was leaving me alone in town without my brother or Jayce there.

Larson had actually been on the phone with Aaron when I called Jayce.

Since I was on speaker phone with Jayce and the others...

Lily overheard everything.

She went crazy when she heard and Larson had to take his phone off speaker to hear Aaron and Jayce over her screaming. It seemed the only way to calm her down was for Stefano to talk to her.

Stefano told her I was fine and he knew I was fine because he knew me. He told Lily I could shoot, I was clever and I was the damn Principessa - so I would be perfectly fine.

I know she was scared, she had just found out our parents were dead–Larson and I are all she has left.

Of course she has the entire Mafia clan as family but I know what she meant.

We talked all the way home as Jayce drove.

Larson built Ravenhall Manor–his and Lily's house here in Paradise Falls the same time as Aaron.

Since he is Aaron's second and they are combining Haven and Paradise it made sense.

I was just glad Lily would be living here in Paradise Falls with me.

She and Larson were supposed to get married in Haven Falls in May of next year but now I don't know what will happen.

Lily and Larson's house is about 3 miles from ours.

When Uncle John and Benny built their homes and the town; they set aside several acres of Paradise Falls for Jayce and Ben.

My dad did the same for Aaron.

The land is about 8000 acres running between both towns...

We all share it together...its home.

We all picked the land on the side of Paradise Falls that had open fields but were beside the vineyards of Haven Falls.

When Jayce and my brother were sixteen they built the houses on the open land turned facing front to the field where our tree stood.

They built the houses at least a mile apart from each other so you could see between them, but you had to drive because they were too far apart to walk.

Standing at our tree and looking at the houses from left to right they are as follows:

Gage: Blackstone Manor

Ben: Grey Crest Manor

Ours: Legacy Meadows Estate

Aaron and Alyssa: Story Brooke Manor

Larson and Lily: Ravenhall Manor.

Ben and Gage both started building their house the day they turned sixteen, it is kind of a tradition in our clan.

All the houses and shops built in the town are made of red cedar log wood inside with sandstone on the outside.

The towns itself looks like a small country town, with fields of grass and you could see the grape and olive vines in the distance.

Only the stores and shops look like the ones from Italy. But that is the only place our parents designed to look like home.

All of the houses look nothing like the ones in Italy...

Uncle Vic's home reminds me of a castle.

All the elders in our clan and their families use to live there together...

Have been for generations...

Well, until my father and the others moved to America.

My father said since they were starting over they would start from the beginning.

All of the men in the clan agreed to build the homes with logs of trees...

Since it was how it was done "in the olden days".

I told you...

My dad and "Uncles" are weird!!

After everyone had eaten we left Cardea Steakhouse...

Jayce and I along with the others headed toward home.

Just before we got to the turn off to head toward our house, I told him to pull over.

Jayce pulled his truck over into a large field with a huge tree growing in the middle of the field. I got out the truck and started toward the tree.

I knew Jayce was following close behind me.

I could hear the others getting out of their trucks.

Just before I reached the tree Jayce grabbed me and flipped me over his shoulder. Laughing as I flipped over in the air and was now head first to the ground.

"Jayce...put me down right now!"

I demanded all the while giggling like a little girl.

"No," was his only reply as he carried me the rest of the way to the tree.

This tree was special…

When I was about seven, I told Uncle John this field needed some trees and asked if I could plant some.

So me along with Jayce, Aaron, Ben, Gage, Larson and Lily came out here and planted about twenty trees.

None of the trees made it except for one.

No matter what we did…

We could not get the other nineteen to grow.

About three years later…

Right after Jayce, Aaron and I had gotten back from Italy we were riding by the field. I yelled for Uncle John to stop the truck.

We all got out looking at the one tree that stood tall in the middle of the field. All around the tree was the pretties green grass but only one tree had survived.

Three years later on my thirteenth birthday…

Jayce brought me out here to this tree.

We carved our names into the tree and he gave me a silver diamond charm bracelet. Over the years, all of the guys had bought me charms for it and now there was barely any room left for anymore.

Over time–other names were carved into the tree that now grew strong in the field in front of our houses.

Larson and Lily's names were carved in the tree on her fifteenth birthday.

Aaron and Alyssa carved theirs six months to the day they met.

Ben and Gage's name are the only ones not there yet.

Jayce has told them they could carve their names in the tree too – but both were waiting.

"The tree has special love powers...you don't mess with things like that..." is what Ben always declares when Jayce or Aaron bring up about them carving their names in the tree.

Ben says that every couple that carves their names in the tree together end up getting married and he is not carving until he knows her name!

I don't know about powers...

But this tree is special and it's ours.

We all sat around talking and looking up at the stars as the sky turned to dusk.

We talked about the old wood box that I found under my bed...none of us could figure out what it was. Of course, Ben thought it was some secret map to the location of treasure or bodies that the elder's didn't want us to know about.

We only knew it had to be important for Victor to have hidden it inside my bed and of course it was locked!

I never had a chance to ask Aaron about the things in the bag that he had taken from my car.

Just before night had completely fallen we all left to go home. Carlos had left after he finished eating to go meet with Uncle Stefano and Costa to head home to Angel Crest Estate.

Jayce and I headed over to our house...the others headed toward theirs.

Jayce and Aaron started building both Legacy Meadows Estate and Story Brooke Manor on July 6…just a couple days after their 16th birthday.

Both were finished and ready to move in almost a year later on June 5th…two days after their high school graduation.

Alyssa graduated the same day, so she and Aaron planned to move most of their things into the house. Aaron was going to keep living at home with me until I had graduated high school.

My birthday was only thirteen days away when Jayce moved in and I was turning fourteen.

Dad said I could go and stay with Jayce for the summer in Paradise Falls.

Jayce and I spent that first night together in Legacy Meadows Estate and Aaron and Alyssa spent their first night in Story Brooke Manor-next door.

It was never a problem for my parents with me staying alone in our house with Jayce. We had slept in the same bed together for as long as I could remember.

Jayce and Aaron would go camping and they always took me along. I always shared a sleeping bag with Jayce, so it was never a big thing.

I know most parents wouldn't let their soon to be fourteen year old daughter stay alone with a soon to be seventeen year old guy-but it was not a big thing in our family.

In our family girls waited until her wedding night to be with her husband. Even if the girl was engaged she remained a virgin until her wedding night. Having a father who would surely kill the boy otherwise-made it a very easy rule to follow and no one ever broke it!

Aaron and Jayce were the only two guys I ever slept in a bed with.

When I was around twelve years old Gage's mom Julianna was killed in a car crash by White Feather.

He shot out the front tire of her car causing her to go head first over the side of a winding road. She was on her way back home from out of town.

When the phone call came Aaron came into my room to tell me. For two weeks, I was too scared to go to sleep and slept in Aaron's room with him.

During those two weeks, my father and the others locked down all four towns and searched for White Feather.

He had disappeared...just like he always did.

When the boys were younger Aaron would have the others come over to Haven Manor for sleepovers all the time–for as long as I could remember they were always together at someone's house. They would always include me in whatever they were doing.

At night we would all camp out in sleeping bags on the living room floor. Once when Aaron and Jayce were thirteen and Ben and Gage were twelve they had planned a special camping trip to Paradise Falls. They were going to camp out in the field where we had planted our tree.

I had just turned ten the day before so they surprised me with the trip! Lily had gone to see her grandparents and wasn't able to go with us.

We roasted marshmallows and hotdogs and the guys all took turns telling me stories.

When it was time to go to sleep Ben had said I could stay in the tent with him and Gage. This of course was not fine with Jayce!

He told his brother that I was staying in his and Aaron's tent...sleeping in his sleeping bag with him, so he could keep me safe. He also informed him that I could only sleep with him because we were getting married.

Jayce took protecting me very serious...even at thirteen years old!

There was nothing out in the field to be afraid of, but Jayce was just being Jayce. After that night, Ben never said anything about me sharing his sleeping bag again.

But when they would stay over at Haven Manor and we would camp out on the living room floor–Ben would always put his sleeping bag beside Jayce's so he would be next to me.

All the guys were very protective over me but Jayce was the worst followed by my brother.

Chapter 5

I went to take a shower and get ready for bed as soon as Jayce and I got home. He had told me to go first because he had a few things to get straight before we left for Haven Falls in the morning.

After I gotten a shower and put on my pajamas I walked into the living room to tell Jayce I was out. He had just hung up the phone when I walked into the room.

"Hey, I'm out of the shower so you can go ahead when you are finished."

I told him as I walked around the sofa to sit down next to him.

"Angel, will you… are you going to be alright going back to Haven Falls tomorrow? I can't tell you anything about what we will find when we get there. I haven't seen all of the video recording from Haven for this morning. Dad told me and Aaron not to worry about it because he and the others were going to watch them. He said Victor was going to watch all the feeds recorded on the flight here. We just have to wait until in the morning…talk to Victor and the others."

I leaned my head back on the cushion of the couch looking over at Jayce.

"Yes…I will be ok as long as you are with me. I will be glad when Uncle Vic gets here and we can figure out what is going on. I am just worried what will be left standing…when tomorrow is over," I told him as I sat there worrying about what would happen.

Jayce kissed my forehead smiling at me before getting up to go take his shower.

I walked over to the fridge to get something to drink before heading back to the bedroom. I crawled in bed and turned on the TV to find something to watch while I waited for Jayce to finish his shower.

I was watching a scary movie I found playing on the movie channel and didn't hear Jayce come back into the bedroom.

On the screen, some guy in mask was chasing some dumb girl who was running in heels. I was telling the girl how stupid she was and that she needed to lose the heels and run like hell. The bad guy went to grab the stupid girl at the same time Jayce crawled into bed beside me scaring me half to death.

I started screaming…

Of course Jayce thought this was funny and started laughing at me.

"Angel…you shoot bad guys without blinking an eye. I have seen you bring a grown man twice your size to tears and you are scared of a movie?"

I couldn't shoot Jayce I loved him – so I did the next best thing. I turned around and punched him dead in the arm.

Now I don't throw a weak girly punch; as well as I can shoot, I can fight. The boys taught me how to fight starting from the time I could walk. I am a black belt in karate and I know kickboxing as well as Taekwondo.

I knew my punch didn't have any effect on Jayce, he is all muscles.

My brother and Jayce had taught me to fight but I could never bring either of them down. Now Ben and Gage were a different story, since I had taken both of them down several times.

They had taught me that even though I was small there was always a way to bring a man down. Just because the guy would always be bigger than me, didn't mean he would beat me.

The bigger they are the harder they fall; you just have to find the right pressure points to bring them down.

Jayce's phone started ringing and he answered still laughing at me.

I could only assume whoever was on the line had asked him why he was laughing. Of course, Jayce proceeds to tell the caller everything that had happened from the time he got out the shower.

I could hear him telling whoever was on the phone what he had said to me.

I turned my head to look at Jayce just as laughter come rumbling from over the phone…I knew exactly who he was talking to.

"Give me that phone right now…I can't believe either of you!"

As soon as the phone was in my hand, I placed it to my ear and began to rant.

"Uncle Vic...I can't believe you are laughing at me! Jayce scared me when he got in bed! I didn't hear him because of the stupid girl on this movie I'm watching. Why do they write movies with dumb girls running around in heels from some bad guy? Why doesn't the girl stop turn around and shoot the bad guy...instead of running? I can't understand why the girls feel the need to be so helpless and dumb. Just take off the damn heels...run like hell, grab a gun and kill the guy."

Of course all I hear in response is more laughter only this time Nick and Buono had joined Jayce and Uncle Vic.

"Well if all you guys are just going to laugh at me...I am giving Jayce back his phone. It is not polite to laugh at somebody!! I can't believe all of you...I am being serious talking about how the movies are written to make girls all helpless and dumb; and all you are doing is laughing at me!"

Uncle Vic finally stopped laughing long enough to talk to me.

"Principessa I was calling to see how you were after this morning. It does my heart good to hear your voice and know you are *sicuro* (safe). I talked to Stefano and I have watched all the feeds from Haven Falls this morning. Your *descrizione* (description) of the men were *percise e informativo* (very precise and informative). You kept calm and did exactly what you should have. I am very proud of you *amore* (love). We will be landing at seven in the morning. John is coming to meet the plane...then we will all be meeting up around eight o'clock. I will see you in the morning Principessa, try and get some sleep tonight. *Ti amo* (I love you) Arabella."

He always tells me he loves me in Italian and never in English.

"I love you too Uncle Vic. I will see you in the morning."

I told him hanging up the phone and handing it back to Jayce.

I turned back to the movie as Jayce called Aaron and the others to let them know what time we were meeting. I overheard him tell them to just meet here at our house and we would all ride together.

The bad guy had killed the stupid girl and was now breaking into the house where she lived in with three other girls. At least one of the girls looked smart, she was wearing tennis shoes so she would hopefully be able to run from the killer.

Just as he had slipped into the room and grabbed one of the girls slitting her throat the other one started screaming. I was telling the girl on the TV to shut the hell up and start running…just as Jayce finished up on the phone.

"Baby…why are you yelling at the TV…you know they can't hear you," he asked me.

Causing me to turn looking at him confused as to why he was even asking.

"Because they are not fighting him…they are just running and screaming. I just want to slap them and tell them to stop acting like some helpless bimbo," I explained since it made perfect sense to me.

Jayce only shook his head reaching over pulling me down until I was lying across his chest.

"So baby…did you like your graduation presents?"

Sitting up confused I looked down at him and asked, "What do you mean presents? The car was my present...is there something else?"

Smiling Jayce asked, "Did you read the note that was in the box with the key?"

I had completely forgotten there was a note in with the key.

Hopping off the bed, I went over to the bag I had put the box in pulling it out and opening the lid. I had seen the note earlier but didn't have time to read it. I told this to Jayce as I walked back to the bed.

"I forgot about the note...you know with trying not to get killed...or kidnapped!"

He just laughed at me as I opening the envelope and removed the card.

The card was from Aaron's stationery that I had made for him for his 18th birthday. It was really nice stationery–I had his name and Haven Falls engraved into the set.

Opening the card I began to read out loud.

Princess,

Congratulations on graduating high school with honors.

Here is the key to your new car.

Jayce and I got everything you asked for inside.

There is also a surprise in the trunk from both of us to complete the look!

Enjoy, I love you Princess.

Love Aaron and Jayce

Before Jayce could say a word I was already up and running out of the bedroom heading to the garage.

I could hear Jayce coming behind me laughing and I started to run faster. I knew if he caught me I would be going to the garage over his shoulder.

When I reached my car, I raised the trunk door I saw the black box tied with a pink ribbon holding it closed in front of me. I reached for the box to pull it out when Jayce reached around grabbing it for me.

The box was a large square box that was a little over a foot tall and three feet wide.

Jayce lifted the present out starting toward the house only to turn around to see I was not following. He sat the present on the steps we had just came down and walked back over to me.

Studying the inside of my car I noticed several different panels within the lining of the trunk.

"Jayce...what is all this?" I asked him.

He reached over to the panel on the right side of the trunk and pushed the small black button. As soon as he pushed the button the right panel slowly began to open. Inside were two 9 mm handguns black with a pink handle and two solid black glocks.

Jayce told me they were there for backup...should I ever need them.

Several clips filled with hollow point bullets were lined up beside each gun.

Jayce then showed me how to release the panel on the left side of the trunk, inside was a state of the art computer system.

"The computer system is linked to our network. You can see any of the feeds from all of the towns by clicking on the town you wish to see. Here is where you click to see the feed for Angels Paradise Falls and...here is the feed to Victor's plane," Jayce explained showing where each feed was.

I clicked on the link to Victor's plane to find Nick sleeping.

"What about our two planes? Is there a video feed for them on here?"

I asked trying to find it on the screen.

He answered pointed to the link on the screen.

"Yes, the link to it is right here below Victor's plane."

You would think with all of us having live feeds to everything, we would have problems with someone breaking into the software. Victor and our parents had taken care of those problem years ago.

I am not exactly sure how they locked the feeds down but I knew it was secure.

After we had shut down the computer and closed all the panels we headed back in the house.

Jayce picked up the box and walked into the kitchen. I closed and locked the door before following him to our bedroom.

Jayce sat the present down on our bed and moved over to let me open it. I untied the pink ribbon and lifted the lid; inside was the black leather jacket and black leather boots that I had asked for.

The boots were designed with a hidden pocket inside the lining at the top of each boot. The pocket in the right boot was big enough to hold my gun securely against my leg. The left boot had a slender thin pocket running from the top of the boot down. This was made to place a dagger or a short blade knife or sword.

The jacket was fitted at the top and flared out around my hips ending just before the middle of my thigh.

I was going to look awesome in them!!

After I had taken the boots and jacket out of the box…

I put them in our closet, while Jayce took the box off the bed. I walked back into the room smiling as I climbed back into bed beside Jayce.

"I love them you know…thank you for getting them for me. I will thank Aaron in the morning," I told Jayce as I laid my head down on the pillow.

Jayce turned to look over at me as he tucked the hair behind my ear.

"Baby I am glad you like it. I want you to be happy. I will do everything in my power to make you happy. I love you Angel."

Looking at Jayce I knew if I was going to get any answers from him now was the time.

"Jayce, will you tell me why the meeting was changed?"

I asked him as I waited patiently for him to explain.

Jayce took a deep breath and started telling me why he had called my brother so early that morning.

"I got a phone call about 5 o'clock this morning. When I answered the caller said that he had seen White Feather in Angels Falls. When I ask him for his name...the caller hung up. I called Aaron first and told him what had happened. He said he was going to tell your father to stay in Haven Falls with you but that he was on his way. I called Stefano...had him check the live feed to see if he could find him. When he couldn't I called Rocco and sent him to Angel Crest Estate.

After Aaron got here Rocco called to say he couldn't find any sign of White Feather anywhere in Angels Falls or Angels Paradise, but was going to stay and have another look around. Stefano thought it would be best to move the meeting to today. Carlos was staying behind with Rocco since Larson was on his way to pick him up. Stefano and Costa had just arrived to Sea Court Manor about twenty minutes before you called me.

When Alyssa heard you telling us about the men you saw in Haven Falls she pulled up the recording of the phone call I received earlier. She listened to the call two or three times before she told us that she was almost certain that Oscar was the one that called me. Dad had pulled up the feeds to Haven Falls while you were talking to me and saw Oscar talking to one of the men you described.

Stefano had called Victor right after I called him this morning but after you called me...he called Victor back. He told Victor you were in Haven Falls alone but we were trying to get you back to Haven Manor...so we could get you out of town. Aaron was on the phone with Larson and was yelling at my Dad he was going back to Haven to get you. Victor told him not to leave Paradise Falls unless we couldn't get you to Haven Manor. I have never seen Aaron so mad…he told Victor if anything happened to you he would kill him."

I was surprised that Aaron had threatened Uncle Vic because in our family we are taught to respect our elders, especially elders of the clan.

I turned to look at the ceiling thinking…before I started talking.

"Jayce I don't understand why now. If Troy or Oscar wanted to hurt or kidnap me…they have had plenty of other chances. Why now? It doesn't make any sense. I know that Oscar called you knowing Aaron would leave to come here. But why say he saw him in Angels Falls…why not here? Do you have any ideas as to why this is happening now?"

Jayce turned my head so I was looking at him and not the ceiling.

"No Angel, I don't. It doesn't make any sense as to why now. The only thing I can think of is that you were leaving to come here. Today was the last day you would be in Haven Manor since you were moving home with me. I am not sure what Troy told White Feather…or even how he knew him. Dad said that as far as he knows White Feather didn't know where we were until Troy told him. Aaron and I think it has something to do with the box from under your bed. Victor and Stefano were really worried about getting you and that box out of Haven Manor. Since none of the elders will tell us anything…we don't know what the box is or what's inside. Don't worry…we will find out what is going on…I promise. You are safe and no one is going to hurt you. I will kill anyone who tries…no one is taking you away from me."

I laid there in Jayce's arms as I drifted off to sleep.

I didn't know what tomorrow would bring or what I would find when we arrived in Haven Falls.

The last thing I heard as I fell asleep…was Jayce telling me he loved me and that I was safe.

Chapter 6

The next morning I felt Jayce carefully get out of bed as not to wake me, it was a rule not to wake me up before 7am.

The rule became official by my father and the others when I was eleven years old.

Mom would always say that I have always been this way for as long as she can remember. She said I started around the time I was old enough to tell them to go away.

You see any time someone would try to wake me up before seven I refused to get up, but was always awake on my own at 7 o'clock each morning. The older I got I would throw whatever was in reach at the person at my bedroom door; which was usually my brother.

I had hit Aaron and Jayce numerous times on the head with books, jewelry boxes and whatever else I could reach.

I have no idea how many things I broke over the years.

Mom told my brother to leave me alone several times but for some reason he and Jayce loved to make me mad.

All that changed when I was eleven...

Both Nick and Jayce were staying over with Aaron and decided it would be fun to wake me up at 5 o'clock in the morning to see what I would do.

Believe me they learned their lesson that day!

I have a huge hand carved wood princess bed...

I always slept in the middle with my pink and black pillows all around. I always put my gun on the pillow beside me facing the door.

All three of the boys decided to come in at the same time...so neither would miss whatever show I was about to give them.

Well they got a show alright!

All three of them snuck in my bedroom...stood by my bed and shouted out loud, "Time to get up Princess!"

I sat up in bed with my gun in my hand and shot all three of them.

Jayce was on the right side so he got a bullet in his left arm.

Aaron was on the left so I shot him in the right arm.

Poor Nick, the unfortunate soul standing in the middle, got a bullet in the leg.

After I shot all three of them...the elders decided that it would be a law not to wake me up in the morning.

We have a few laws and I will tell you more about them later.

There are not many but is best to obey them...

Nothing crazy–like one is about how the guys can't shoot each other when they are fighting.

That rule came about when Ben and Gage were fighting and Ben won. Gage wasn't happy with the way Ben was gloating about how he won–so Gage shot him in the shoulder.

The rule the elders came up with for me was:

No one is to wake up Arabella before 7am in the morning. If you do, you do so at your own risk. If this rule is disobeyed results could lead to severe injury or death.

Besides I have no idea what could possibly be a reason anyone would need to get up before seven in the morning.

You see I have a theory…no one agrees with my theory but it is what I believe.

Schools don't start until 8am and businesses don't open until 9am; so if you get up at 7am that gives you thirty minutes to get ready and thirty minutes to get to where you need to be. Besides what is so important it can't wait until eight o'clock or at least 7:30 at the earliest?

I am the only sane person around here I believe.

Everyone I know…including my best friend gets up at six o'clock every morning.

I ask you, what do you need to get up that early for? What are you going to do for two hours before the workday starts?

It makes absolutely no sense to me what so ever! Your body needs sleep!

I woke up to the smell of coffee and could hear voices coming from the kitchen. I crawled out of bed and went to get dressed.

When I walked in the kitchen I saw Aaron sitting at the table beside Alyssa. I went over and sat on his lap, hugging him tightly.

"Aaron thanks for my presents I love them. I love you too big brother."

I told him as I smiled up at him.

He just laughed and kissed the top of my head before telling me to go get my coffee.

I got up and walked over to Jayce, giving him a hug and a kiss on the cheek before taking the coffee cup from his hands.

Just then...the front door opened and Ben and Gage walked into the kitchen.

Ben came over giving me a hug and kiss on the forehead before going to fix his cup of coffee. Gage sat down beside Aaron and watched as I walked back over to the table.

I went to sit in the chair beside Alyssa only to have Jayce sit instead, pulling me down on his lap.

I watched Gage as I drank my coffee waiting for him to tell me what was wrong. Gage gets quite when something is bothering him and he usually tells us when he is ready.

This morning though he just sat quietly and watched me.

After I had drunk the entire cup of coffee and he still hadn't spoken a word–I knew I was going to have to say something since it seemed like he wouldn't.

"Gage, are you going to sit there all morning staring at me? Or you want to tell me what is going on?"

Everyone at the table stopped talking looking back and forth between me and Gage.

When Gage didn't answer me I turned and looked over at Ben for an explanation. Ben just shrugged his shoulders at me as he looked between Gage and the others.

"Arabella, I don't know what is going on with him this morning. I tried to get him to tell me what was wrong on the way here...but he hasn't said a word."

Worried about Gage, I got up and walked around the table to where he was sitting.

Before I could ask him again what was wrong; he jumped up out of his chair grabbing me in his arms. Gage wrapped his arms around me hugging me tightly against his chest. No one in the room said a word as they all just sat there in shock.

"Gage you have to tell me what is wrong. I can't fix the problem if I don't know what it is. Talk to me."

Finally Gage looked down at me.

"Peanut...White Feather killed my mom and he almost got you. I still have my dad but you lost your mom and dad. I don't know why he is here or even how he found us. I want to kill him so bad.. I don't even know who he is. How can I protect you from someone I don't even know?"

I could see Gage was worried and scared. He took the death of his mother hard and it took months before he didn't want to kill everyone in his path.

"Gage you don't have to worry about protecting me by yourself. We will all protect each other just like we always have. We are all stronger together...we will all be ok. I promise. White Feather is not going to get me because none of you will let him. We think Troy told him where we are but we don't know what he is after. Uncle Vic and the others know more than they are saying...I think it's about time they told us what the hell they know. Don't you?"

Stepping back and sitting down in the chair he looked over at Jayce.

"Jayce...Peanut is right the elders know a hell of a lot more than they are telling us. I talked to dad this morning...asked him what was going on. He won't tell me anything...just said to meet them at Sea Court Manor this morning."

Aaron looked over at me asking, "Princess are you going to be alright going back to Haven Falls?"

I just nodded my head yes, as I walked to put my cup in the sink.

Aaron turned to say something to Jayce...just as my phone starting ringing.

I answered the phone and heard Nick's demanding voice loudly in my ear, "Arabella, are you ok?"

I told him I was fine and ask him where they were.

"We just got to Sea Court Manor. We are pulling up the drive now. Are you on your way here yet?"

I told him we were leaving Legacy Meadows and would see him in about twenty minutes before telling everyone it was time to go.

We walked outside and got into the truck and headed toward Sea Court Manor. Aaron and Alyssa were riding along with us since Alyssa was staying behind with Marie.

Ben and Gage took Ben's truck following behind us.

I could see Larson's truck coming down their driveway and waved at Lily as we passed by. Larson pulled his truck out behind Ben and together we all headed out toward Sea Court Manor.

We drove up the lane just as John came walking out of the house with Victor.

I looked over at Jayce and then back at my brother.

"This doesn't look good. Is it just me or do they look like they are hiding something?"

I asked them looking out the window to where Victor and John were talking.

Aaron leaned forward to look out the window at them and then looked at me–he turned back to Jayce.

"Jayce, I think it's time for you and me to have a little chat with them. They are hiding something big and I think we need to find out what."

Jayce pulled up and turned off the truck. He watched as his dad and Victor disappeared around the side of the house.

Before he could answer Aaron the front door opened and Nick came running out the house. He headed straight for us as we all got out of the truck.

Ben and Gage were walking over to me looking at Aaron and Jayce.

Ben looked at Jayce asking, "Hey what are you all looking at? Why are you both standing there staring at the side of the house?"

Jayce turned toward Ben just as Nick walked over pulling me in his arms for a hug.

Aaron was the one that began talking and explained to Ben and everyone else what we had seen.

When Jayce asked Nick if he knew anything he replied, "I don't know what to tell you. Dad has been acting crazier than usual...since Stefano called him yesterday. He was on the phone with Stefano most of the flight here. Then as soon as we get here...he and John start whispering in the corner. When I ask them what was going on they took off outside."

"Well this is just great! It's not like we don't have enough problems with Troy and Oscar...not to mention we have no idea how or why White Feather is here. Nick is he still here? Did you see the video feeds with Uncle Vic? Does he think White Feather is still here or has he disappeared again," I asked Nick.

Nick just shook his head as he squeezed me tighter.

"No Principessa, he is not here anymore he's gone now I promise. I did see some of the video feed but not all of it. I saw where he killed your parents...you both have my condolences."

Aaron told Nick thanks and we all headed toward the house. Just before we could get to the door, Uncle Vic and John came walking back around the house.

Uncle Vic came over and gave me a hug and kiss on the forehead before leading all of us inside.

As soon as we got in the living room Uncle Stefano and Costa said it was time to go.

Uncle Benny picked up a bag and handed it to Victor before we left the house.

Jayce's mom Marie handed out sandwiches, a cannoli with drinks for all of us before kissing Uncle John good-bye, telling us all to be careful.

Lily was staying behind with Alyssa and Marie. Lily came over to hug me and reminded me not to forget anything from her house. Larson and I were going to pack her things and bring them back with us.

Alyssa and I had already moved all our things to Paradise Falls two weeks before.

Larson had moved in Ravenhall Manor about six months ago.

Alyssa hugged me and told me to be careful then kissed Aaron goodbye just before we left.

We drove to Haven Falls with me holding my hands under my legs to keep from shaking.

Nick and Aaron had rode with us and were talking with Jayce the whole way there. I wasn't listening much, I was thinking about what we would find...when Haven Falls began to appear outside my window.

I could see the houses and shops just ahead.

There was not a single person around...it was scary quiet.

I looked over at Jayce as he turned down the street heading toward the sheriff station. I turned and looked back at my brother and Nick to see both of them reaching for their guns.

Jayce pulled across the street from Haven Sheriff Station and parked. Larson pulled up beside us and Rocco stepped out followed by Ben and Gage.

The elders had all rode together in John's SUV.

After everyone was out we all started toward the station.

I could see my dad lying in the street ahead where he fell when he was shot...

The closer I got I could tell something was very wrong.

I started walking faster to see where all the blood had come from at the end of his arms.

Just I as was close enough to see him...

I saw someone had cut of both his hands and left white feathers in their place.

I stepped forward and went to bend down beside him; when I was grabbed around the waist and lifted off the ground. Before I could struggle Uncle Vic put me down several feet away from my father's body.

Victor told us all not to touch the bodies or get near any of the white feathers...they were dipped in poison.

How he knew that I had no idea...just add it to the list of things the elders were hiding.

Victor led us all to the back door of the Sheriff Station before having me stand in front of the door and place my hand on the pad by the door. Within minutes of my hand touching the pad I could hear the locks disengage.

I looked over at my brother to see if he knew about the keypad but he just shook his head no.

Uncle Vic and the other elders went inside leaving the rest of us trailing behind. I saw Uncle John going into my father's office while the rest of them turned around facing us.

Victor told us to go to Lily's house and pack her things then come straight back to the station.

We were not to go anywhere else...

Especially not Haven Manor.

Uncle Benny and Costa were going to Haven Manor for my mother's body, so she could be laid beside dad when the town exploded.

White Feather and his men had killed everyone in Haven Falls.

Uncle Vic said it was too many bodies to bury and this is what my father would have wanted.

I only wish Troy and Oscar along with White Feather and his men were going to burn along with my parents and the town that I loved.

We packed up Lily's things and loaded them in Jayce and Larson's trucks before returning back to the station. Just as we pulled in the parking lot Uncle Benny came out of the station heading toward us.

I asked him about my mother and father since his body had been moved from the street. He told me and Aaron that Victor had put them together in my father's office.

Uncle Benny told us that we were to go on ahead to Paradise Falls...

They would be shortly behind us.

I asked him why they had cut off my father's hands. He told me they tried to use them to open the locks here and my bedroom at Haven Manor. He said they would not work on the count of the fact my father had programmed all the locks to only open to me.

Victor had me place my hands on another keypad in my father's office earlier; behind a hidden door in his bookcase that unlocked the entire town including Haven Manor.

We left and headed back toward Paradise Falls.

Uncle John's truck came in to sight about thirty minutes later and he flashed his lights at Jayce.

Jayce and Larson both slowed down and pulled their trucks over on the side of the road.

Uncle John pulled his SUV to a stop in front of Jayce's truck. Uncle Vic got out and walked over to my window. I rolled the window down as he walked up and told all of us to sit tight.

Just minutes after he turned to head back to the SUV the ground shook violently.

I turned around in my seat and looked out the back glass as smoke rose in the air behind me where the houses and shops in Haven Falls had once been.

Nothing remained but fire and smoke, soon to be ash and rubble of my childhood town. Only the vineyards and Haven Manor remained.

I looked at Aaron and the others in shock…

"I can't believe they blew up the whole freaking town! I mean I knew they would but to actually see it. I just can't believe they did it.   Guys they just blew up a whole town!! What the hell are they going to do if White Feather comes to Paradise Falls… blow it up too?"

They all assured me everything would be fine.

Jayce told me they were not going to blow Paradise Falls and even if they did, our houses wouldn't be affected since we lived so close to the vineyard.

Like that is supposed to make me feel better… oh well… at least I know our houses will still be standing even if everything else does go up in smoke.

Uncle John pulled back on the road and started toward Paradise Falls with us following behind.

Nick and the guys talked about their party and the things they wanted to do while we were in Italy.

I asked Aaron and Jayce what was going to happen with the wedding and they assured me that it was still set for my birthday.

I listened as the three of them talked as I watched out the window as we made our way home.

Everything had changed…

I just wondered how much more would never be the same.

Chapter 7

The morning of my 16ᵗʰ birthday I woke to find Jayce

standing in the kitchen cooking breakfast. I walked up behind him and wrapped my arms around his stomach squeezing him in a hug.

"Guess what today is?"

I asked as I stepped back and walked over to the fridge. He just turned and smiled at me.

"Happy birthday, Angel...I am making us breakfast before we have to get ready. I have a surprise for you too."

I got the milk from the fridge and made us both a cup of coffee and then set the table. I turned and looked at Jayce as he filled both plates with food.

"What surprise are you talking about," I asked him as I began to eat.

"You have to wait until the wedding to find out. Don't look at me like that. I promise you will love it Angel," he told me before eating his breakfast, all the while smiling like the cat that ate the canary.

After breakfast I went to take a shower while Jayce cleaned up the kitchen.

I heard the phone ringing just as I stepped out the shower.

I dried off and put on my bathrobe before going to look for Jayce. I found him in the living room talking on the phone…but he hung up just as I walked in the room.

"Who was on the phone," I asked.

Jayce just smiled at me and shook his head.

"Sorry can't tell you baby. It's a surprise. Don't worry you will find out soon. I'm going to take a shower. I love you Arabella."

He told me as he kissed my forehead and walked to our bedroom.

I followed behind him and headed to the closet as he shut the bathroom door behind him. I reached in the back of the closet for the white bag my wedding dress was in and took it out.

I laid the bag across our bed and pulled down the zipper pulling the dress from the bag.

I loved this dress the first time I saw it in the shop in Italy. It is a beautiful floor length lace white dress with thin spaghetti straps made of diamonds with a princess bodice.

Jayce is wearing his black Italian suit and his black dress shoes.

Jayce walked out of the bathroom and headed to the closet to get dressed.

I had just finished slipping on my dress and shoes when the doorbell rang. He told me to answer the door while he finished getting dressed.

I opened the door and was shocked to find Uncle Vic and Nick standing on my front porch dressed in their black Italian suits.

"I can't believe you are here! Why didn't you tell me you were coming?"

I stepped back to let them come inside as Nick looked me over.

"Arabella you look beautiful! We couldn't miss your wedding Princess. Happy birthday, we wanted to surprise you!"

He leaned down to kiss me on the cheek as Uncle Vic stood beside him looking at me.

Uncle Vic took me by the hand turning me around in a circle.

"Principessa, *si guarda bella* (you look lovely). I wish Carmin was here to see you today. I would be honored if you would allow me to stand in for him. Arabella, it would be an honor to give you away today."

I told him I would love for him to give me away as I tried to keep the tears from falling.

Jayce walked over and put his arm around me smiling as he asked if I liked my surprise. I told him I loved it and we all left together to head over to the field where our tree stood.

We had decided we wanted to get married by the tree...

We had carved our names in years earlier.

Uncle John was standing in for Alyssa's father since our dad was his best friend. I had thought Uncle John was walking with both of us but I was very happy to have Uncle Vic walk me.

After everyone had arrived the ceremony began.

Jayce stood next to our names on the left side of the tree...

Aaron stood on the right next to where he and Alyssa's names were carved.

Uncle Vic and John walked Alyssa and I up to the tree and placed our hands in our soon to be husband's hand.

I noticed the mahogany box that I had gotten from under my bed was leaning against the tree on the grass...

Lying on the ground between us on a satin pillow leaned up against the tree.

After everyone was seated the wedding started and I looked into Jayce's eyes as I said my vows.

After the priest pronounced us both man and wife Jayce kissed me before he said, "Happy birthday my beautiful wife. I love you Angel."

Aaron and Alyssa were smiling as the priest told Aaron he could kiss his bride. Aaron smiled at me just before he led Alyssa toward the car.

Jayce helped me in my car before closing the door and climbing in the driver's seat.

We all headed to Cardea Steakhouse for the reception.

After the reception Victor and Nick left to fly back home to Italy since they had to get back to the vineyard.

A week after the wedding I was sitting on the front porch of Legacy Meadows talking to Alyssa and Lily about our upcoming trip to Italy.

We were telling Lily about the shop where we had both bought our wedding dresses since she still hadn't found one she liked.

We were planning which shops we wanted to go to; when I heard the phone ringing in the house. I got up and went inside to answer the phone and as soon as I said hello the caller hung up.

Thinking it was a wrong number I turned to go back on the porch when the phone rang again. I picked it up and could hear breathing coming over the line but when I said hello they hung up.

Alyssa and Lily came walking inside just as the phone started ringing. This time I had Alyssa answer and as soon as she said hello the caller hung up on her too.

I told Alyssa, "Whoever is calling is going to be sorry if they don't stop. That's the third time in a row they called and hung up."

Just as I finished talking the phone started ringing so Lily answered it.

The caller hung up again.

I knew I should call my husband, but he and Aaron were gone out of town and wouldn't be back until later.

The phone started ringing again...

So I answered.

"Hello. I can hear you breathing so I know you are there. Either you tell me what the hell you want or stop calling my house!"

Just as soon as I finished talking…the caller hung up.

Lily was pacing back and forth in the kitchen looking out the windows.

Reaching for my cell phone I called Rocco and told him what was going on. He told me not to answer the phone just as it started ringing again…that he was on his way over.

The phone continued to ring over and over and was still ringing when Rocco walked in the house twenty minutes later.

"It hasn't stopped ringing since I called you! It is driving me crazy. Can I answer it now?"

He told me to pick up the phone and had me say hello while he stood beside me with his ear close to the phone. As soon as I said hello the caller hung up.

Rocco told me he would answer it the next time it rang which was just minutes later. Rocco picked up the phone and as soon as he heard the heavy breathing began yelling into the phone.

"I don't know who the hell you are but I promise you…if you don't stop calling here I will find you. I will find you and I will kill you slowly!"

Just as Rocco spoke his last word the caller on the phone hung up.

Rocco put the phone down and walked over to me putting his arm around my shoulders. He asked what had happened. So we told him how we each tried answering but every time the caller hung up never saying a word. He told me not to answer the phone and to turn on the answering machine.

We have an answering machine but we only use it when we are out of town.

He stayed for about an hour to make sure we were ok but the caller didn't call back...so he left. He made me promise to call him if the caller called back and to tell Jayce and my brother as soon as they got home.

Ever since I was alone in Haven Falls...

Jayce always makes sure either Larson or Rocco stayed behind when they are out of town visiting with vendors.

Lily and Alyssa decided to stay with me until the guys got home. We settled in on the couch to watch movies and eat popcorn.

This is where my husband found us when he got home.

Aaron and Larson walked in the living room with Jayce and sat down on the couch.

We told them about the phone calls and how whoever it was didn't call back after Rocco answered the phone. They weren't sure who it was but Jayce told me to leave the machine turned on for a while.

We all left and went into town to Julianna's Diner.

Uncle Benny had built the diner for Julianna when they built the home and shops in Paradise Falls. She loved to have all of us kids come in and she always gave us milkshakes with extra whipped cream.

The diner had the best cheeseburgers and home-style cut fries in all four towns. Julianna's friend Sue took over running the diner after she was killed.

Sue's husband Gino runs Gino's Pizzeria and he makes the best deep dish pizza. I have told him it tastes like the pizza from Italy which never fails to make him smile.

We had just sat down when Ben and Gage came in and walked over to sit down with us.

Jayce was telling them about the phone calls when Sue walked over to bring us our food. She had made my milkshake with extra whipped cream and winked at me as she gave it to me.

Ben asked her why mine was the only one with extra whipped cream and she just smiled as told him she liked me more.

This made Jayce and my brother start laughing; as Ben tried to take my milkshake.

I just looked at Ben and told him if he touched my milkshake I would shoot him.

Gage was laughing so hard at Ben pouting; that Ben reached over and shoved him on the floor.

After we had all finished eating we told Sue thanks and that we would see her later. She just smiled and waved as we all walked out the diner and headed home.

The morning of Lily's birthday…

I drove into town to Julianna's Diner to check with Sue to make sure everything was ready for the party tonight.

As kids (and even now, since we refuse to grow up)…

We always ate at the diner for our birthday.

Julianna always made the kids milkshakes with extra whipped cream with our cheeseburgers and my mom always made the birthday cake. We would have a party and open presents with family and friends.

Since mom was gone Sue had told me she would take care of the cake.

I went in the diner and saw the cake Sue had made Lily. It was beautiful and she even put the small lily flowers on it, just like my mom used to. Sue and I talked for about an hour while I sat and ate a turkey sandwich and drank my milkshake.

Just as I was leaving, Jayce called to tell me they would be leaving the vineyard around four and should be home by five that afternoon. Jayce and my brother had taken over running the vineyard and handling all the vendor orders when they turned eighteen.

Ben and Gage also worked at the vineyard–helping run the day to day operations.

I left the diner and stopped by the station to see Marie. She helped answer the phone and pretty much ran everything at the Paradise Sheriff Station. She always says that John and Benito just like to play cowboys, as sheriff and deputy as they strut around town.

I walked in the door and found Marie at her desk on the phone. She waved me over as she hung up the phone.

"Hey Princess what are you doing here? Is everything ok?"

Marie asked me as I walked over to sit down beside her.

"Everything is fine. I just left the diner. I was checking with Sue to make sure everything was ready for the party tonight. Just thought I would stop in and see how you were before I head back home."

"Oh, everything is just fine Princess. John and Benito are out playing cowboys doing their rounds around town. It's been quite today…sit and talk to me a few minutes," Marie told me as she smiled.

I stayed and talked for almost an hour before I left to head home.

Uncle John and Benny came back to the station right before I left. They both told Marie and I about how their rounds were good and that everyone was nice and safe in Paradise Falls.

Causing Marie and I to start laughing as they told us how their presents alone was enough to scare a blind man to walk straight.

Still laughing when I got in my car to head home to Legacy Meadows…

Just as I pulled out on the road and started home, my phone rang. I pushed the button to answer the call trying to stop laughing as I said hello.

Ben was calling to see where I was and to check up on me. He wanted to know if I needed any help with Lily's party but I told him I had it covered.

I talked to Ben and then Gage, after he took the phone from Ben to talk to me too. I told them I would see them later at the diner for the party and hung up.

My husband came home at four just after I had got out the shower. I got dressed while he took his shower and then sat on the bed watching TV. I had just got into a new movie when the phone started to ring. I reached for the phone forgetting I was supposed to let the machine answer it.

I answered the phone still watching the movie when I said hello. No one answered me and all I could hear was breathing. Realizing it was another one of the prank calls I got up to go find my husband. I walked into the bathroom just as he stepped out the shower and handed him the phone never saying a word.

Jayce took the phone and listened for a minute before he began to threaten whoever was on phone.

"Whoever the hell you are...I will find you and when I do I'm going to kill you. I am going to kill you very slowly and painfully. So if you are smart you will either tell me what the hell you want or stop calling my house."

Jayce listened a minute to see if the caller would answer...

Then he hung up.

Jayce handed me back the phone asking if I was ok. I told him I was fine, handing him his towel and going back to watch the movie.

After Jayce was dressed I grabbed Lily's present and we headed to the diner.

The party was a success and everyone had a great time.

Lily loved her cake–she almost cried when she told Sue.

It was the first birthday cake not made by my mom.

Lily loved her presents. Sue even gave her sprinkles on her milkshakes...which for us was a treat.

After the party Marie pulled me to the side to talk to me.

"Arabella...you did wonderful and I know Annabel would be proud. You pulled off a great party."

My mom and Julianna were the ones who always planned out our birthday parties when we were kids. After Julianna died my mom took over the planning with Sue's help.

When we got back home Jayce went to his office to make a few calls for work and I went to get ready for bed. I put on my pajamas and crawled into bed and turned on the TV.

Lying down on my side of the bed, I shifted to get comfortable and pulled the cover up reaching over to turn off the lamp. I started watching the TV trying to stay awake but fell asleep just a few minutes into the show.

Jayce came in the bedroom just as I was dosing off. He undressed then crawled in bed beside me pulling me in his arms as he turned off the TV.

"Baby I am so proud of you. Your mom would be proud of you too. You did a wonderful job...I love you Angel."

Jayce told me as he held me rubbing his hand up and down my back.

Looking up at Jayce half asleep I smiled and told him I loved him too before falling back to sleep.

The next morning I woke up, ate breakfast and got dressed before finishing packing for Italy.

We were leaving for Italy the next day.

Jayce had left to go finish up some last minute paperwork at the vineyard.

I had just finished zipping up our suitcases when I heard the doorbell ring. I opened the front door and found Stefano standing on my front porch.

"Hey Uncle Stefano I didn't know you were coming over. Come in. I was just finished packing for Italy. I really wish you and Uncle Costa was going with us. Did you want something to drink?"

I asked him as he sat down on the sofa in the living room.

"No Princess, I am fine. I came over because I wanted to see you and I need to talk to you about something," replied Stefano patting the cushion for me to sit down.

Just then the phone started to ring.

"Princess the phone is ringing. Go answer it I can wait," Stefano told me as he looked from me to the phone.

"I'm not supposed to answer it."

I told him just as the machine picked up and heavy breathing could be heard before the machine cut off.

"Arabella, what is going on? Who the hell was that?"

Stefano asked getting off the couch walking over to the machine.

"Well, I don't really know who it is. This is the third time he called. Or I think it's a he...but I'm not sure since whoever it is never says a word only breathes then hangs up. The first call was the week after the wedding, the day Jayce had gone to meet the vendors–then I didn't get another until last night before the party. I thought after Jayce told him off last night that the calls had stopped. Don't look at me like that I thought Jayce would have told you!"

I replied as he looked at me, not at all happy with what I had told him.

I could see he was thinking something...

I was sure I wasn't going to like.

"Jayce shouldn't have to tell me things like this. Arabella you should have called me right away for all we know this could be Troy making these calls. I need to go," Stefano said as he kissed my head and rushed toward the front door to leave.

"You are leaving? You just got here and I thought you came to talk to me?"

I asked just as he walked out the door and onto the porch.

Stefano turned to me and I could see the worry lines on his forehead.

"I need to talk to John. I promise to call you later Princess."

Not sure what to say all I could do was hug him goodbye. Before he left he made me promise to not answer the phone and to call if anything else happened.

After Stefano left the phone rang twice but I let the answering machine pick up.

I hated to admit it...

I hadn't even thought about Troy but I hated the fact Stefano could be right more than anything.

I knew Troy and Oscar were still alive somewhere but I had really hoped they were smart enough to leave and disappear.

I cleaned up the house to keep my mind occupied and off of whoever was making the calls.

Several hours later...

My doorbell rang again.

I went to the door and this time found Stefano along with John standing on my porch.

After they listened to the messages and I told John the same thing I had told Stefano –he had us all sit down in the living room.

"Arabella, why didn't you tell me about the phone calls when you were at the station yesterday?"

I told him I didn't get the phone call until last night, right before Jayce and I left to go to the party.

"Arabella you need to tell me these things Princess. I promised Carmin that I would look after you if anything happened to him. I agree with Stefano...Troy or Oscar could be the one making these calls, if so we need to be careful," he told me as he looked over at Stefano.

Looking at the two of them so worried...

I wondered if White Feather had anything to do with the phone calls.

"Uncle John you don't think White Feather is calling here... do you?"

I asked him wondering if White Feather even knew I no longer lived in Haven Falls.

John just shook his head.

"No Princess I don't. It's not his style and calling to scare you is not going to help him get what he wants... " he said as he looked from me to Stefano realizing what he had said out loud.

"What is White Feather after Uncle John?"

I asked hoping he would give me an answer this time but of course that didn't happen.

I looked over at Stefano...hoping he would tell me but he just shook his head too.

Before I could ask them anything else the front door opened and Jayce and Aaron came running in the living room. Uncle John had called Jayce and my brother and told them both to meet him here right away.

Jayce came over to sit down by me and Aaron sat on my other side as John started talking.

"As you know Stefano and Costa were planning on staying here with Benito to take care of the winery while we all were in Italy. But with these phone calls you have been getting Arabella...well...we think it will be best if I stay here as well. I know Marie and I planned to fly to Italy and come back home next weekend...but I think we all need to stay after what happened in Haven Falls. I know Rocco and Carlos are planning on staying and that's fine, since Larson will be going with you. I know all of you will be protected in Italy. Buono will protect all of you–especially you Arabella so I think it will be fine for Rocco to stay. I agree with Stefano I think it could be Troy making these phone calls."

Jayce and Aaron talked to John and Stefano and agreed that Rocco could stay behind since I would be well protected.

Stefano told Aaron that Rocco and Carlos would be taking all of us to the airstrip and seeing us on the plane…to make sure we were safe.

Stefano had called Victor after he left Legacy Meadows and told him about the calls. Victor and Buono would now be meeting the plane when we arrived in Italy.

Rocco and Carlos had come to America with their fathers after Nick's mom was killed. Rocco's father–Rinaldo was my father's and John's Capo for our two families.

In our family the Capo was the family hit-man and high ranking protector for the clan sometimes called the right hand.

Carlos's father Dante was the Capo for Stefano and Costa. Carlos took his father's place after he died four years ago when Carlos was only 21 years old.

Rinaldo was killed by White Feather–when he was visiting Buono in Italy since his health was failing, two years before.

Rocco was 23 years old when his father was killed but he had already taken over as soon as he turned nineteen after Rinaldo was diagnosed with cancer.

Rinaldo and Dante had both trained with Buono and the three of them had been friends all their lives. White Feather had killed both Carlos and Rocco's mothers a year before he killed Nick's mom.

I told Jayce and the others I was going to finish up some last minute things before we left tomorrow and left them alone to talk. Honestly I didn't want to hear any more about Troy or Oscar.

I really wanted it to be a great trip but I was sad that John and Marie wouldn't be with us for their son's birthday.

Of course thinking about the fact that Troy could be the one calling and also the one causing problems, only made me mad.

Plus I couldn't figure out what White Feather wanted and it seemed that neither John nor Stefano had any intentions of telling us.

After I had finished packing everything I went to the kitchen for something to drink and a snack.

John and Stefano had just left moments before I finished packing.

Aaron and Jayce were standing in the kitchen talking so I asked them if they wanted something to drink. They both said that they did, so I fixed them a glass along with mine and sat down at the table.

"So...everything ok?"

I asked them looking back and forth between them-trying to read their moods.

"Angel everything will be fine I promise. Try not to worry," Jayce said kissing me on the cheek all the while smiling down at me.

My brother asks me if John or Stefano had told me anything else before they got to Legacy Meadows.

I told them about how John had said White Feather wouldn't be the one calling...

Because it wouldn't get him whatever he was after.

Aaron stayed about an hour before he left to go home and help Alyssa finish packing for tomorrow.

Jayce took both of our suitcases and placed them by the front door before declaring he wanted to take a shower.

He picked me up and threw me over his shoulder as he headed toward our room…

All the while, telling me that taking a shower together would save time and water.

It never saved time when we took a shower together…

But it was always fun.

After we were dressed we got ready to leave since we were all meeting up at Cardea Steakhouse.

It was tradition…

Anytime we left for a long trip to Italy the whole family got together.

We would be gone for a month this time and it would be the first trip without any of the elders going.

Lily was excited about going to Italy since she had never been before. She listened closely as Stefano was telling her the places she needed to see while we were there.

Chapter 8

The day we were leaving for Italy arrived...

At ten that morning Jayce loaded our bags in Rocco's car before we left to go pick up Ben and Gage.

Carlos was picking up Aaron and Alyssa first then getting Larson and Lily and meeting us at the plane.

When the elders built the towns they built a small airstrip and plane hangar in Angels Paradise.

The small airstrip was big enough to land and take off in our planes which were always prepped and ready.

No matter the circumstances.

Costa and Stefano had designed the hangar large enough to house both our planes; as well as Victor's when he came to visit. We had two private jet planes that belonged to the vineyard here in America; but Victor had at least four back in Italy.

The small plane was big enough to sit ten passengers and the cockpit sat two pilots. The large plane was big enough for thirty passengers and had four separate bedrooms with six bathrooms.

After everyone bags were loaded on the plane Rocco told us to have a safe trip before going to talk to the pilot.

Rocco and Carlos both got their pilot licenses six months after they turned twenty-one–they took over for Rinaldo which was the elders' pilot.

Usually when we go anywhere Rocco or Carlos always fly the plane but since they were staying behind this time…Benito had called his friend Henry to fly us to Italy.

We were taking the small plane since there were only eight of us going. Henry was going to fly us there then he was bringing the plane back home.

We would be flying home in a month and Victor was having one of his pilots bring us home.

When Henry shut the doors to the plane and started toward the cockpit he stopped. He told us to call if we needed anything before closing the cockpit door.

Jayce sat down on the couch and pulled me down next to him. He always sat beside me anytime we got on a plane since we were kids. Usually Aaron sat on my other side but this time he and Alyssa took a seat on the couch in front of us.

The plane had two long couches facing each other along the inside of the plane. At the back of the plane was a bathroom and to the front a TV was mounted on the wall beside the cockpit door.

We use to sit on our knees with our faces squashed up against the windows when we were kids, as we took off and landed.

Ben and Gage sat on the couch with me and Jayce both fighting over who would sit next to me.

My husband told them to either take turns or he was switching seats with me and they would have to sit next to him the whole flight.

I just laughed as they played rock, paper, scissors…

Ben sat pouting when Gage won the first half of the flight.

Lily and Larson sat on the couch with Aaron and she could not sit still, she was so excited. Larson told her she was going to have to calm down or he was going to tie her down, so she wouldn't hurt herself.

Everyone just laughed as she tried to sit still only to start bouncing in her seat; before Larson would look at her and she would stop.

After we were in the air for a couple of hours all the guys went to the bar to get something to drink. They got comfortable in the recliner bar stools and starting talking.

Jayce had bought me something to drink earlier that I finished just before I fell asleep.

Flying has always made me sleepy and Alyssa was the same way.

Lily was sitting on the couch watching TV with Gage and Ben when I fell asleep.

An hour before we landed I woke up to find Alyssa and now Lily asleep.

I got up and walked over to Jayce and took the glass from his hand drinking. I sat down in his lap and listened to them talk as I laid my head on his chest.

Just before we landed Henry called the phone to tell us we would be landing in the Italy soon.

Larson went and woke up Lily before sitting down and pulling her in his lap.

Aaron didn't wake Alyssa as he picked her up and sat down with her in his arms.

As soon as the plane touched the ground Alyssa opened her eyes and looked out the window behind her.

I walked over to see what she was looking at...

As she continued to stare out the window eyes wide.

There on the tarmac was Victor and several armed men standing beside five large SUVs.

The sight was quite scary looking...

Well not to me but you know...

I guess other people, maybe.

I looked at my husband's amused face and started laughing so hard...

Everyone turned and looked out the left side of the plane.

Alyssa and Lily both looked worried, at the sight of at least eight armed men with guns along with Victor and Buono.

I was laughing so hard when the plane finally stopped, I fell to the floor. Ben was the closest and reached out to pull me up.

Lily looked at me and then the others before she turned to me eyes wide; as she switched from shocked, scared and now confused looking at me.

"Arabella...uh...there are a lot of men standing out there with guns and you are laughing. Please tell me this is the punch line from some joke because I don't see what is so funny."

Lily and Alyssa both looked from me to everyone else as I tried to stop laughing...

Seeing that they were both truly scared and shocked, I started toward them.

I walked over to Lily and sat down on the couch beside her.

I looked at Alyssa and then turned to Lily patting her hand.

"There is nothing to worry about I promise. All of the men outside work for Victor...so we are safe I assure you. This is the first time all of us flew to Italy...you know without at least one of our parents. So...since Carlos or Rocco didn't come with us Uncle Vic brought extra protection. We are safe I promise you...plus you know we are all armed. This is just Victor making sure we are safe. Ok?"

Lily and Alyssa both shook their head trying to understand what I was saying...

I knew they weren't scared anymore but I could still see a little hesitation.

Ben smiled at both of them declaring that I was right this was just Victor.

Henry opened the plane door telling us all to have a good vacation, as we headed down the stairs toward Victor.

As soon as I stepped off the plane Buono was waiting for me. He told me that all the girls would be riding with him so the boys could talk shop, but I knew he really wanted to talk to me about something.

I walked over to Victor with Jayce and the others. Victor held out his arms for me as I walked up to him.

"Buono has something he wants to tell you love, so you are riding back with him," Victor whispered in my ear.

I stepped back and looked at Victor's smiling face and knew it was something good.

Victor told Jayce and the others they would be riding with him so they could talk and the girls would ride with Buono.

Jayce kissed me before he helped me in the car before turning to go get in the car with Victor.

Alyssa and Lily sat in the seat facing Buono and I as the driver headed toward Tesori Cove Villa.

"So Buono what did you want to talk to me about?" I asked.

Buono turned to me smiling. I could see whatever he wanted to tell me was really good news.

"Oh Arabella…it has finally happened. I do believe we have a wedding soon in the future. Nick and Francesca have finally realized what I have been telling them for years. They are destined to be. I don't know why it took them so long but they are in love Princess."

Looking at Buono beaming face I just laughed as I told him.

"I told you to leave them alone and let nature take its course. You can't push them together…you have to let love grow on its own. Just look at me and Jayce it took me longer to fall in love with him. Just leave them be…or you will just cause problems I keep telling you!"

Buono just smiled at me and shook his head as Lily asked, "Who is Francesca?"

Turning to look at Lily I told her, "Francesca is Buono's daughter, she's seventeen and you will get to meet her as soon as we get to Uncle Vic's. Buono has been saying her and Nick would get married since they were little. Nick and Francesca grew up together and have always been friends…but this one here has been pushing them together for as long as I can remember. I think they started really liking each other as more than friends about two years ago. I told Buono to leave them alone or they would never end up married."

Buono just laughed and turned back toward me winking as he said, "We are having a tea party while you're here Princess. There is a new little café in the village that has the best cannoli and tea biscuits. You know Victor will want to go…and you girls are welcome to join us."

He said to Lily and Alyssa as he turned to look at them.

Lily and Alyssa were looking at me and then Buono quite confused.

"We always have a tea party with Arabella…when she comes to Italy ever since she was ten years old. I remember the first tea party was right after she shot me in the arm…because I was rude. I remember looking down at the cutest little girl with her blond curls holding a pink gun still pointed at me after she shot me. She wanted me to teach her how to shoot. That day was the first of many lessons. Over the years I have watched her grow into an incredible young woman, who is a damn fine shot with a gun in her hands."

Buono looked like a proud father as he starting talking about when I was younger…looking at him made me realize I might have lost my father but Buono had always been a spare father to me.

Lily and Alyssa just sat and listened as Buono had told them some of the stories that had happened over the years with me and the guys growing up.

Just as he finished telling them a story about how I was the first girl to really learn to shoot in our family…

Lily turned and looked at him confused.

She looked between me and Buono before she began to question Buono.

"You mean Arabella is the only girl that can shoot. None of the other women can shoot? I thought her mom and Marie could shoot a gun?"

Lily asked as I watched the wheels in her head turn trying to figure out how she never knew this.

Thing is…

I can't remember if I ever told Lily.

It just never came up.

Buono explained that my dad and the others taught my mom, Marie and Julianna how to shoot a gun after we moved to America.

My mom and the others could shoot…

But only well enough to try to defend themselves, should they need to.

Women weren't taught to shoot a gun.

The men were the ones who protected them. There was never any need, so it was never done.

Until I came along, girls didn't touch guns let alone know how to shoot to kill like I did.

I was still the only girl in our family clan that even carried a gun and knew how to shoot.

I know for a fact, that women are not allowed to touch a gun in the other two Mafia clans...

No women at all, it just wasn't done not ever.

I know it has always been kept quite that I can shoot a gun – only our family knows and not even all of them, I think.

Anytime the women left they always had a protector with them.

Dante was Julianna's protection, when they both were killed four years ago in the car crash caused by White Feather.

Lily asked Buono why we had moved to Italy and he began to tell them the story about how we came to live in America.

Buono sat back in his seat getting comfortable as he began the story.

"In the family clans, when a child is one and a half years old, they have a christening with their family and love ones. At Nick, Jayce and Aaron's christening...White Feather killed Nick's mom. To be sure that Jayce and Aaron were safe...the others moved to America taking our greatest treasures to hide from White Feather. They left only days after the funeral...in the dead of night so that White Feather would not know where they were going. White

Feather killed so many of our love ones and we wanted to keep the rest safe."

As he finished the story I started to ask him what White Feather was after; just as Angels Paradise Falls came into view.

We pulled in the drive and started down the lane toward Tesori Cove Villa.

It was just as beautiful as I remembered.

When the house came in view Lily gasped, "Arabella it's beautiful! It looks like a castle."

I had always thought the villa looked like a castle from the first time I saw it.

Just as the cars pulled in front of the house...

I saw Nick and Francesca standing there waiting for us.

Buono opened the door and helped me step out just as Nick picked me up swinging me around laughing.

"Arabella, you're finally here. Princess I get you for a whole month! Can you believe it?"

Looking up at Nick as he put me down, I smiled up at him.

"Hi Nick. I guess you are happy to see me, huh?"

Nick looked over behind me smiling; talking to whoever was walking up behind me.

"I am keeping Arabella."

Turning around I saw Jayce and the others walking over toward us.

"You can't keep my wife. She is already taken Nick," said Jayce walking over to pull me next to him.

Francesca came over to where we stood and reached out to hug me.

"He has been driving me crazy Arabella. I am so glad you are here. Granddad is really excited to see you…he wants me to bring you by soon," said Francesca as she reached over to hug Jayce too.

I told her I couldn't wait to see Giovanni. I had missed him.

Giovanni was Buono's father but he had been like a grandfather to all of us kids growing up. He was the sweetest man you could ever want to meet. At 76 years old he was the oldest man living within our families.

My father, Victor, John, Stefano and Costa all lost their parents when they were young. So we never had any grandparents.

After we had unloaded our bags from the cars we started toward the front door.

Lily leaned over to me and whispered, "Arabella…I knew all of you were rich but I never realized you were…castle rich!!"

Smiling I looked at Lily and grabbed her hand whispering, "Just wait until you see the inside."

I always knew we had money but I never really cared and I was glad Lily didn't either.

But I know she didn't realize just how well off we are…

Until, she saw Victor's home.

I knew it wouldn't change anything between us. Since, neither of us never really cared about money. We just love each other for who we are. She was a true friend and I never doubted that fact –as I watched her eyes widen as she looked around.

Lily eyes widen so much I was afraid they would pop out her head, as she saw the inside of Tesori Cove Villa for the first time.

I could hear Alyssa laughing behind me as she watched Lily's head jerk back and forth as we toured the villa.

She kind of reminded me of the dash board big eyed bobble heads! It was funny.

The inside was beyond beautiful–with wood floors and tall stone walls. The staircase curves up toward the two top floors where the bedrooms are, each with large private suites and balcony.

Just to the left of the front door was a large living room with a large stone fireplace surrounded by windows overlooking the vineyard.

On the right and down the hallway there was a large kitchen and dining room–which held a handmade large mahogany table, which had been in our family for generations.

As we walked toward the back of the house–two double glass doors opened to the veranda with seating surrounding a stone fire pit…the vineyard could be seen for miles.

After we had put our suitcases in our bedrooms; we all headed down to the kitchen to see what Ms. Rosa had made for supper. Ms. Rosa had been Victor's cook and housekeeper ever since Nick was born.

She made the best homemade lasagna I had ever eaten and my mom always loved it too. We walked in the kitchen to find her taking the three large pans from the oven.

"Hi Ms. Rosa, something smells wonderful," I said walking over to her.

She turned around smiling before she held out her arms.

"Oh Arabella...come let me look at you love. You look so much like Annabel did when she was your age. Now who is this lovely young lady?"

Turning around in Rosa's arms, I introduced Lily just as the others walked in the kitchen.

Aaron went over and hugged Rosa before trying to swipe a piece of her homemade garlic bread; before she swatted his hand with her wooden spoon.

Everyone sat around the table together eating and talking. Even Giovanni came over to join us. We all talked until almost midnight before we all headed to our bedrooms to turn in for the night.

The next morning Lily, Alyssa, Francesca and I met up with Rosa to help her finish up the food preparations for the party.

She showed Lily and Alyssa how to make the caprese salad which had fresh mozzarella, tomatoes and green basil seasoned with salt and drizzled with olive oil. Yum...

Francesca made the Focaccia Milanese; which is flat bread covered with Italian ham, goat cheese, oregano, garlic, and fresh tomatoes. I helped Rosa with the pasta and I made homemade biscotti and butter cookies.

I always loved helping mom bake for her café when I was younger.

Victor had ordered the three birthday cakes from a shop in town.

After we had finished with the cooking, Rosa told us to go outside and sit on the veranda and enjoy the sunshine.

We spent the rest of the day talking and planning which shops we wanted to go to over the next few weeks.

On the morning of Jayce's birthday I woke to find workers decorating the veranda for the party that afternoon.

Nick was sitting at the kitchen counter when I walked in the kitchen.

After Rosa had handed me a cup of coffee I went to sit down by Nick.

"Nick where is Jayce and Aaron this morning?"

I asked him as I sat drinking my coffee.

He told me they had rode over to the wine barrel warehouse with Victor.

After I had finished my coffee Nick asked me if I would take a walk with him.

We were walking along the grape fields when Nick turned to me and said, "Arabella, I have something I want to show you."

Reaching in his front pants pocket Nick pulled out a small blue box that he placed in my hand. I opened the box to find a beautiful 3 carat round shaped diamond surrounded with a halo of small diamonds engagement ring.

"Nick it is beautiful! Francesca is going to love it! When are you planning to ask her to marry you?"

Nick took the ring back closing the lid before putting in back in his pocket.

"I thought I would ask her tonight at the party. Do you think she will like it?"

I just smiled at him as I slipped my arm through his as we headed back to the house.

"Nick she will love it. I promise. You know Buono is going to be ecstatic! I am so happy for you both. I love you and I love her for making you so happy," I told him as the front of the house came into view.

We walked in the kitchen to find all the others sitting at the table eating butter cookies and drinking coffee.

I went and sat in Jayce's lap after giving him a birthday kiss as Nick sat beside Francesca.

Francesca told me that Giovanni was coming to the party tonight and that he said he wanted a dance with me.

Jayce asked me where Nick and I had been and I just whispered that I would tell him later.

We all sat around talking about the party…

Francesca was telling Lily and Alyssa about some of the shops we needed to visit while we were in Italy.

That night we all gathered around the veranda…

We ate the food we had helped Rosa fix and sampled a piece of each of the three birthday cakes. We talked and laughed to almost midnight before the party finally came to a close.

Nick asked Francesca to marry him and she said yes as she jumped up and down; as Buono declared that we needed champagne to celebrate. Everyone was cheering as Nick slipped the ring on Francesca's finger.

Giovanni told everyone that the news called for a dance, as he winked at me.

Just before the party was over Larson pulled Nick aside to ask him if he could tell him where the nearest jeweler was.

Later that night as we got ready for bed Jayce told me that Larson was going to ask Lily to marry him while we were in Italy.

Nick had told him about the jeweler he had used and where he could go buy the rings.

Over the next week, Lily toured the estate and met the workers as she got to see how the wine was made.

Jayce and the guys met with Victor to go and meet with several new vendors. They would all work during the day at the winery while the girls and I when into the towns to shop.

Two weeks after we had arrived in Italy...

Alyssa, Francesca and I took Lily to the shop where we had bought our wedding dresses.

Larson had proposed to Lily two days after the party and gave her a beautiful 2.5 carat round solitaire diamond.

Lily found the perfect dress and was talking to me about her wedding. We had just left the shop and stopped in this small café to grab lunch.

"Arabella, I was thinking about maybe just getting married while we are in Italy. Since my parents and Haven Falls are gone…I know the wedding we planned will not happen. I was talking to Larson last night and he asked me if I wanted to go ahead and get married. What do you two think I should do?"

Lily asked Alyssa and me as we sat drinking our cappuccinos.

Alyssa told her if she really wanted to get married that Victor could probably set something up. Lily asked me if I would talk to Victor and see if it would be alright to get married at Tesori Cove Villa.

I talked to Victor the next day and he told me it would be fine. And of course, that he would set everything up.

We had planned the wedding for July 29th the day before we left to go back home to America. With only a week before the wedding, Alyssa, Francesca and I helped Lily find dresses for us to wear to the wedding.

Since Jayce, Aaron and Nick had packed their suits to bring to Italy–only Larson had to go into town to buy a suit. Nick and Aaron took Larson to the shop where they bought their Italian suits to have one made for Larson.

Two days before the wedding…

Alyssa and I headed into town to pick up the dresses and Larson's suit.

Francesca had stayed behind with Lily to help Rosa prepare the food for the wedding. Victor had called and ordered a cake and was having it delivered the morning of the wedding.

Alyssa and I had just loaded the dresses and Larson's suit in the car. We were walking over to pick up an espresso before heading back to the vineyard.

Just as we started up the street toward the café Alyssa grabbed my arm; pulling us behind the front window at a small shop.

I turned to ask her what was wrong, when she pointed out two men that she said had been following us.

I didn't recognize either of them and I was sure I had never seen them before.

I watched as they looked around, trying to find where we had disappeared to. Looking around the corner as not to be seen; I took my phone and snapped their picture just before they stepped inside the café.

I grabbed Alyssa's hand as soon as it was clear and we ran back to the car.

I started the car and pulled out on the road, as Alyssa looked to see if the men had seen us.

"Arabella...do you know them...do they work for Victor?"

Alyssa rambled all in one panic breath.

I took my gun and laid it beside me–as I pulled the car on the road and headed back to Tesori Cove Villa.

I shook my head at Alyssa as I swerved between cars.

"No they don't work for Victor. I don't know who they are."

Looking behind us as we passed the café, I saw both men walk out and look in our direction. The two men ran and jumped inside a large black truck and began following us. They were speeding up behind us, getting closer racing to catch us.

I reached for the button on the steering wheel and dialed Jayce as I tried to keep ahead of them.

Just as Jayce answered, the truck sped up hitting us in the back bumper of our car.

"Arabella what happened? What was that noise? Did you hit something?"

Jayce's voice demanded loudly as I tried to answer him and think of a way out of this mess.

There was no way I could make it back...

They were going to cause us to crash if I wasn't careful.

Trying not to run off the road I sped up as I tried to stay ahead of the truck.

"Jayce we are being followed...the truck just rear ended me. I don't know who they are but two men are following us in a black truck...they are trying to run us off the road."

I heard Jayce yell for Aaron and Nick...

As Alyssa sat beside me, gripping the seat as she watched the truck speed closer to us.

"Angel just hold on we are coming!"

Jayce yelled as I heard the truck sped up just before it rammed us in the side.

Alyssa was yelling for me to go faster...

As the truck gained on us and slammed into the driver side again, hard enough to shake me.

Aaron was yelling for us to tell him where we were…

Alyssa was trying to tell him as I stepped on the gas swerving trying to get away from the truck.

Just as we got to the outside of the town, the truck pulled up beside us trying to cut us off.

Nick was yelling at Jayce to drive faster…

Aaron was telling us to hold on they were coming.

I saw the road ahead that lead to the villa and took a sharp turn to the right.

Jayce and the others were still at least five miles away…

As I raced to get to them before the men got us killed.

I told Jayce they needed to hurry because I didn't know how much longer I could hold them off.

"Arabella…" Alyssa screamed just seconds before the first bullet hit the back window.

"Jayce they are shooting at us…I don't know how long before the back window crashes," I yelled as four more bullets hit the window.

"We are coming Angel…just hold on baby…." Jayce pleaded as bullets continued to rain against the back glass.

Trying to keep from crashing…

I drove as fast as I could as bullets hit the car, rattling my bones.

"Princess we are coming now. Buono and dad are right behind us," Nick told us just as the back window shattered loudly.

I yelled for Alyssa to get down...

As I swerved to keep the bullets from hitting us – or worse kill us.

I so wanted to kill both of them...

But I had to get Alyssa somewhere safe.

Just as I saw Jayce and the others come into view...

A bullet took out the back driver's side tire.

I could hear Alyssa screaming and yelling at Aaron to help...

As the car started to spin I grabbed the steering wheel trying to keep us from flipping over.

I could hear the gunshots coming from behind us...

They were coming from in front of us...

I looked up to see Buono aiming at the truck and firing.

Just before we crashed...

I slammed on brakes as I pulled the car over to the left side of the road.

I grabbed my gun and turned...

Just as the driver of the truck stopped behind me, he was getting out followed by the second man.

I could see Jayce and the others speeding to us...

I knew they wouldn't reach us in time.

I told Alyssa to stay down as I opened the passenger door so we could get out. Just as we stepped out I grabbed her pushing her behind me–as I turned around and pointed my gun toward the men.

I pulled the trigger taking out the driver...

The second man kept shooting at us.

Just before he could pull the trigger again...

He fell to ground when a bullet hit him on the left side of his head.

Looking over behind me...

I watched as Jayce jumped out the truck and ran towards us.

Nick was holding the gun he just shot the second man with still pointed at the bodies...

He walked over to them.

Aaron came running over pulling Alyssa is his arms; as he turned to check on me, at the same time.

I told them we were fine and ask who the men were that were trying to kill us. Nick stood over the bodies as Victor and Buono checked their pockets for ID.

Buono and Victor loaded the bodies in the back of the truck before Buono left driving the truck...with Victor following.

Nick came over to me with his gun still in his hand.

"Princess, you two ok?"

I just looked at him and nodded before asking if he knew who the men were. Nick told me they were hired hit-men but he didn't know who they were working for.

Jayce took my hand and led me back to the car I was driving before shutting the door after I had sat in the passenger's seat. Aaron and Alyssa got in the truck Jayce had driven. Nick crawled in the back of the car with us after he and Jayce changed the tire.

We all started back toward Tesori Cove Villa as Nick and Jayce were trying to figure out who had hired the men.

We pulled in the drive of the villa and I got out grabbing the suit and dresses.

I turned and informed everyone that Lily was to know nothing about what had happened before her wedding…

Before turning to head inside with Alyssa following me.

We walked in the kitchen where Lily and Francesca were helping Rosa finish up the food.

Alyssa and I didn't want Lily to know about what had happened…

Since she would want to leave right away and we didn't want her to miss out on having her wedding tomorrow.

I gave Francesca her dress and handed Lily Larson's suit as Alyssa and I headed upstairs to put our dresses away.

The rest of the afternoon we helped finish up the last of the preparations for the wedding.

Francesca's grandfather, Giovanni came over and had supper with us that night. He wished Lily and Larson much luck in the future and promised to attend the wedding.

He asks me when I would be having a little one and I told him it would be awhile.

Victor laughed as Jayce answered as the same time as me. Only he had told Giovanni that it would be soon.

I just looked at Jayce like he was crazy as he told Giovanni to expect a little boy come next July.

Chapter 9

Lily's wedding was beautiful…

She and Larson walked down the aisle together.

Aaron and Jayce both had offered to walk her down in place of her father, but she and Larson decided since neither had parents living anymore they would walk together.

I stood beside Lily with Alyssa and Francesca standing beside me. Aaron was Larson's best man and Jayce and Nick stood next to Aaron.

Victor had transformed the garden in the villa…into a fairytale with twinkling lights hanging from trees.

Lily cried as the priest pronounced them man and wife. Larson wiped her tears as he leaned down to kiss her.

After the ceremony we all walked to the veranda to dance and eat.

Lily and Larson cut their cake as we all stood around cheering and laughing.

Around midnight we all headed in to pack and get some sleep before we left the next morning to board our flight home.

I had just finished packing when Jayce crawled into bed patting the bed beside him as I walked over. I slipped under the covers beside him as he turned out the lights before pulling me in his arms.

"Well, I thought the wedding turned out wonderful. Lily seems happy and I know Larson is glad to finally have her as his wife. I hate that it happened this way without either of their parents but everything worked out."

Laying my head on his chest I told him, "It was beautiful and Uncle Vic did a wonderful job. Lily and Larson are happy and that's all that matters. I love you."

He told me he loved me too. As I drifted off to sleep I could feel him kiss my forehead.

The next morning we all loaded up in the cars...

To head to the airport and fly back home to America.

I had already told Francesca good-bye and was hugging Nick before we left.

"Nick did you ever find out who hired the hit-men?"

I asked wondering if he had heard anything.

He told me he didn't know yet, but that he would call me as soon as he found out. Nick told Jayce and the others good-bye as we climbed in the cars and headed out.

We all climbed on Victor's plane and settled in as the plane took off toward home.

Aaron and Jayce were talking to Larson about what had happened when Alyssa and I were in town...

And of course Lily overheard them talking.

She turned to look at me and then Alyssa before she threw her hands up and started yelling.

"What are they talking about Arabella? Why didn't you tell me what happened when you got back to the house? Why are hit-men trying to kill you and I know nothing about this?"

Alyssa took her hand as she explained what had happened, trying to calm Lily down. When she asks us who had hired the two men to kill us, we told her we didn't know…yet that is.

Aaron explained to Lily that Victor and Buono were working on finding out who had hired the men. Aaron told her that as soon as he found out Victor would be calling to let us know.

This seemed to satisfy her as we sat back together to watch a movie on the TV.

The plane touched down at Angels Paradise and John and the others were there waiting.

As soon as the doors opened Rocco came over to help us down. Rocco held out his hand for me as I climbed down the stairs.

I stepped down from the plane next to Rocco…

He grabbed me pulling me in a hug, "Arabella I am so glad you are safe. Princess, this is the last time you go off without one of the men when you are Italy. I am so sorry I wasn't there but Jayce told me you did very well. I am proud of you for the way you handled the situation but no more running around Italy alone."

I smiled up at Rocco as I told him I was fine hugging him tightly before I reached over to kiss him on cheek before stepping back.

He still insisted that I had to have someone with me…

Smiling as he informed me that it would be better if he just went with me instead. I just shook my head and laughed as I walked toward the others.

Uncle John and Stefano weren't much better…

They fussed over me declaring that I wasn't to go out alone anymore. They even hinted at a full time bodyguard!

I of course told them, that was ridiculous and that I didn't need a bodyguard because I could take care of myself.

When we finally arrived home to Legacy Meadows…

I was beyond tired and I had missed home.

I told Jayce all I wanted was a hot bath and to lay in bed with him.

We were trying to decide on what movie to watch as he pulled in the garage.

We unloaded the bags and walked inside the kitchen through the garage door.

Home never looked as good as it did when we walked in our bedroom.

Jayce went to check the machine since the light was blinking as I put the laundry in the basket.

The messages begin to play as we both listened.

The first couple of messages were from some vendors asking for Jayce to call them back. Mostly boring work stuff, so I tuned it out as I unpacked our bags.

Just as I thought it was finished…

The machine beeped to play the last message.

I turned to look at Jayce as Troy's recorded voice began to play.

"Seeing as how you will be dead and not hearing this message Arabella. This message is for you Jayce. I am very happy to tell you that the reason your wife and Alyssa were killed is because of me. I wanted to tell you that since you stopped me from getting Arabella in Haven Falls…I have decided to take her away from you. Aaron shouldn't have married Alyssa she belonged to Oscar. He took much pleasure as he helped me find the two hit-men that killed her. You should have never married Arabella…she was mine! White Feather might have failed in getting what he was after…but I did not. I'm just sorry I had to kill her because I could have had so much fun with Arabella. Well this is good-bye…and again I hope you suffer right along with Aaron."

I looked at Jayce shocked, before turning around running through the house to make sure all the windows and doors were locked.

I could hear the phone ringing as I ran back in the kitchen.

I stopped just as I reached for the phone scare to answer, turning around to look at Jayce.

He walked by me as he reached over and picked up the phone.

"Yeah...we got one too. Yes...I know. No... Troy was the one that left the message. Ok...I will see you in a few minutes."

He hung up the phone before he looked over at me–telling me that it was Aaron that called.

"Aaron told me that Oscar had left a message like the one we had from Troy. He and Alyssa are on their way over here. He said you need to talk to Alyssa...she is really upset. I need to call dad and find out what he wants to do. Angel...call Rocco and tell him to come over," Jayce told me as he tried to smile to hide the worry showing in his eyes.

I walked over and wrapped my arms around him, as I began to shake.

He held me close telling me everything would be ok.

I walked back to the bedroom to get my phone as Jayce reached in his pocket for his. I could hear him talking to his dad as I dialed Rocco.

The phone only rang once before Rocco answered, "Princess, everything ok...what's going on?"

I sat down on the bed trying to figure out how to even answer that question...

Before I begin talking, I tried to quiet down the running thoughts of how I wanted to kill Troy and Oscar.

"Rocco we need you to come over here now, please. We know who ordered the hit-men…that tried to kill me and Alyssa. There was a message on the machine when we got home. It seems Uncle Stefano and John is right about Troy making those calls. Troy called while we were gone and left a message for Jayce. He is the one…along with Oscar that tried to have us killed. The thing is…he seems to believe it worked…he thinks that Alyssa and I are dead. Aaron called, he is on his way over and he got a message too…but his message was left by Oscar."

Just as soon as I said we knew who ordered the hit-men…

I could hear him start up his truck while I was talking. I knew he had already started this way before I finished telling him what was happening. So I knew he would be here soon.

"I am on my way now. I will see you in a minute," Rocco told me before saying good-bye and disconnecting.

I hung up the phone and walked back in the kitchen just as the doorbell rang.

I went to open the front door since Jayce was still on the phone. As soon as I opened the door wide enough…

Aaron rushed right by me and headed straight in the kitchen where Jayce was still talking on the phone.

I took Alyssa by the hand and walked her in the living room. After I told her to sit down, I headed to the kitchen to get her something to drink.

Just as I walked in the kitchen, my brother reached over to hug me as I walked by. I told him I was fine and asked if they wanted anything to drink.

I fixed the drinks leaving Aaron's and Jayce's glass on the counter next to them as I headed back to Alyssa. I handed her the glass as I sat down next to her; telling her everything would be fine.

I don't know who was more angry–me, her, or our husbands. I knew the others would be furious when they found out about the phone calls.

After twenty minutes we heard the front door open as John and the others walked in.

Alyssa and I sat back on the couch as we heard the others walking toward us.

Uncle John and Rocco came in followed by Jayce and Aaron. Stefano, Costa, Gage and Ben came walking in shortly after.

Stefano was on the phone with Victor, as he sat down across from me. Stefano handed me the phone only saying that Victor wanted to talk to me.

After I assured Uncle Victor that I was fine and that we were all safe – I handed the phone to my husband. Jayce talked to Victor and Nick for a few minutes before hanging up and handing the phone back to Stefano.

Everyone was arguing back and forth, trying to figure out what to do.

Nobody could agree with so many suggestions…

Hunting both of them down…

Torturing and/or maiming them in some way…

Before killing both of them slowly…

To some weird things that didn't even make sense.

I knew everyone was angry and we weren't solving anything the rate we were going, so I decided I had enough.

I spoke up getting everyone's attention.

"What if we do nothing? No…hear me out. For some reason Troy and Oscar both believe that Alyssa and I are dead. Maybe we should wait and see how long before they find out we aren't. Alyssa and I aren't planning on going out of town anytime soon…."

I was saying before Alyssa interrupted to declare that we wouldn't be going anywhere anytime soon.

I smiled at her as I turned to the others before continuing to explain my reasoning.

"As Alyssa was saying…we aren't leaving town so we know that we will be protected. Everyone in town knows to look for Troy and Oscar…and they know to call you Uncle John if they see them. I don't know why they think we are dead. I guess they don't know we killed the hit-men either. Maybe we should wait and see what happens. If they call again or show up anywhere…then we can do something about it then. I don't know about all of you…but I am not going to let either one of them dictate how I live my life."

Jayce just smiled down at me as he put his arm around my shoulder pulling me close to his side.

Ben and Gage both agreed that they thought we should wait and see what happens.

Uncle Stefano and Costa both looked impressed at what I had said.

Uncle Costa told me that was a very grown up way to look at the situation.

After all of them had talked it over and Stefano had called Victor to see what he thought of my idea, they all agreed.

I told everyone in the room not to call Larson or Lily and tell them until tomorrow. I told them all if any of them called and ruined their first night in Ravenhall as a married couple; they would have to answer to me.

Everyone left shortly after with Alyssa feeling much better than she had when she arrived earlier.

Jayce shut and locked the front door behind them and turned to take my hand.

He walked me to our bathroom where he filled the whirlpool tub with hot water and bubbles. He came over and kissed me as he reached to grab two towels.

After we were both undressed…

We crawled in the tub together and I closed my eyes as we shifted to lie back for a while. Jayce rubbed my shoulders while we alternated between talking and closing our eyes.

We tried to decide what movie we wanted to watch but we were still having trouble agreeing on one. I told Jayce I was hungry when my stomach started talking–wanting food…he told me he would order a pizza from Gino's when we got out.

It didn't take long before we finally decided on the movie just as the water was starting to cool. We both got out of the tub. I got dress in my pajamas while Jayce slipped on his pajama pants reaching for his phone to call in the food.

I settled under the covers, after I had turned off the bathroom light as Jayce went in the kitchen to get us something to drink.

I turned on the TV and started the movie just as he came in the room and crawled in bed beside me. We sat watching the movie about forty-five minutes before the doorbell rang–with the promise of food.

Jayce went to get the door and I went to the kitchen to grab some napkins.

Jayce walked back in the bedroom with the pizza box in his hands, as I reached for it. He crawled back in bed and started the movie again as we sat watching it and eating pizza.

After the movie was over he took the empty box as I grabbed our glasses to take back to the kitchen. When we finished cleaning up we headed to bed.

Four days later on August 3rd ...

We all went to Julianna's Diner to celebrate Gage and Ben's 17th birthday.

Sue had made them both a chocolate cake and decorated it just like my mom used to. Everyone had a great time and the boys loved all of their presents.

Just before we left to go home...

Sue pulled me over to the side to talk to me.

"Arabella...I know Alyssa's birthday is coming up in three weeks and I wanted to ask you what kind of cake she likes."

I told her we needed to ask Alyssa before I turned and called out to her.

"Alyssa, can you come over here a minute?"

She got up from her seat and walked over to where we were standing. I ask her what kind of cake she wanted for her birthday and she told Sue what kind she liked.

After the party was over and everything was put away and cleaned; we all left to go home.

The next two months went by...

Everything was quiet. Life carried on peacefully.

We didn't get any more phone calls. It seemed that Troy and Oscar still believed we were dead.

The only surprise we did get was a phone call from Nick telling us him and Francesca had eloped on September 14th.

Buono and Victor were beyond happy even without getting to throw a large wedding. They both were already asking when they would be grandparents.

October rolled around and we celebrated Uncle Benny's 37th birthday. It was just the family here since Victor and Nick couldn't fly in.

Uncle Benny said he only wanted to get the family together at the diner. He loves and misses Julianna. It seems his birthday is when it hits him the most that his wife is gone.

Larson 19th birthday followed on October 17th and we all celebrated at the diner with milkshakes and sprinkles for everyone.

Of course it was only just us kids...

Well none of the elders were there...

So it was just us that night.

Victor, Buono, Nick and Francesca flew in from Italy on October 19th. We had planned a huge party for Stefano and Costa's 39th birthday.

Since they had grown up together and shared their birthdays...they always got one large cake together.

Victor had asked them one time why they didn't get separate cakes...

They told him that they were destined twins only born to separate mothers. They have always been close and have lived together for a long time. They are best friends and always had been. If I didn't know any better, I would swear they were twins they were so much alike.

Two weeks after the party on the morning of November 4th I woke up feeling sick. I got up and tried to eat only to throw it back up.

Lily called me later that morning to tell me she was coming over but I told her not to. I told her I was really sick. She asked if I needed anything but I told her I was sure it was only a virus.

I was sure...

Alyssa had it too and had called me earlier to see if I was sick like her.

The next week both Alyssa and I stayed in, as we tried to get better.

Alyssa slowly did start to feel some better but I was so sick I could barely walk.

But on the morning of November 14th after we had both been sick for two weeks—we decided it was time to go to the doctor.

Jayce had called the day before and scheduled mine and Alyssa's appointment. He and my brother decided we had been sick long enough and needed to go see Doc.

I woke up that morning to get ready to go – Rocco was taking both of us. Jayce and Aaron had gone out of town to meet with a vendor and couldn't be there to drive us.

Rocco was going by to pick up Alyssa first before he came to get me.

The doorbell rang and I slowly went to answer the door...

Just trying to put one foot in front of the other, I was so weak.

When I opened the door and stepped back, a dizzy spell hit me taking me to my knees.

Rocco grabbed me just before I could hit the floor.

"Arabella...are you ok? Hey what's wrong?"

I told him I was dizzy probably because I couldn't keep anything down.

Rocco picked me up in his arms and turned to shut and lock the door. Before, putting me down in the front seat of the car and shutting the door.

I laid my head back as another dizzy spell hit...

Alyssa leaned forward in her seat, "Arabella...what's wrong are you ok?"

I turned my head to look at her as the spell passed and asked her if she had been dizzy at all.

She told me no. She had only been extremely nauseous and was having trouble keeping anything down.

Rocco started driving toward town as he listened to us talking. Alyssa thought maybe since I was so small that whatever this virus was, it was hitting me harder.

I closed my eyes as another dizzy wave hit me and told Rocco not to call Jayce until after I had seen Doc. He promised to wait; since we didn't need them trying to get back here and get in an accident.

Rocco pulled up at the doctor's office and parked before walking around to lift me from the car. I told him I could try to walk but he and Alyssa were afraid I would fall and get hurt.

The nurse asked why I was in Rocco's arms and he told her about the dizzy spells. The nurse told him to go ahead and take me on to the room, so I could lie down.

Alyssa was in the room next to me and Rocco went to the waiting room to sit and wait for us.

I closed my eyes as I heard Doc's muffled voice through the walls and knew he was in with Alyssa.

I had just fallen asleep when Doc walked into the room to check on me.

I tried to sit up but was hit with another dizzy spell that almost sent me falling off the table.

Doc had the nurse come in and draw some blood and hook up an I.V. in my arm. He told me I was severely dehydrated and that Alyssa was next door getting an I.V. also.

As soon as the bag was almost empty I began to feel much better.

I sat up on the bed, just as the door opened and Alyssa walked in. She asked me if she could wait in the room with me for Doc to come back with our test results.

She said she was feeling much better too since her I.V.

The nurse came in the room to find both of us sitting up talking and unhooked the I.V. from our arms. She told us that Doc would be with us soon.

Doc walked in shortly after she left and ask Alyssa and me if we wanted him to give us our results together. We both told to go ahead as we waited for him to tell us what was wrong.

He smiled at both of us and told us we were both six weeks pregnant...

Both of us due sometime around the first of July!

Alyssa looked from the doctor to me and started laughing.

Doc gave us both some vitamins. He told me I had to eat more and that I needed to drink more fluids. He was concerned with me being so small about the dizzy spells but said he would keep an eye on me. He told me I should start gaining weight now with the vitamins–but if I didn't gain any soon, he would change me to another type.

Doc told Alyssa she should be fine now that she was no longer dehydrated; but she needed to eat and take care of herself. She told him she knew she had gained a little weight but she thought it was all the sweets we had eaten in Italy.

We both thanked him and turned to walk out of the room toward Rocco. Rocco stood up as we approached him and ask me if I was feeling better. I told him I felt much better and ask if he would swing by the diner to get me a milkshake before we went home.

Alyssa told Rocco he could just drop her off at my house. She was just going to stay with me until Jayce and Aaron got home. Alyssa assured him we were ok. She told him that we were both dehydrated so Doc gave us both I.V. fluids and some vitamins.

Rocco dropped us both off a Legacy Meadows and made us promise to call him if we needed anything.

I unlocked the front door then Alyssa and I walked inside. Alyssa turned to me and started laughing again–as she told me that our husbands were going to be very surprised.

Aaron and Jayce both thought that Alyssa and I had a bad virus so they weren't expecting to find out we were having a baby.

Alyssa and I sat in the living room looking at magazines–we had picked up on the way home of maternity clothes and nursery furniture.

Lily called to check on us and we told her we were doing much better and would see her tomorrow.

Jayce and Aaron called on the way home to check on us.

I told him we were both lying on the couch waiting for them.

About an hour later, we heard the front door open as my husband and Aaron walked in the living room.

They both came and sat down beside us asking what Doc had told us.

Alyssa looked at me and started laughing again...

She was laughing so hard tears were pouring down her face.

All I could do was sit there looking at her like she had lost her mind.

Aaron looked from his wife to me before asking, "Princess what did the doctor tell you two...why is my wife laughing?"

Jayce looked over at Alyssa-who was still laughing.

Jayce and Aaron waited for me to talk as I reached for Alyssa's arm. I tried to get Alyssa to calm down but every time she tried to tell them anything...

She would try to talk only to start laughing all over again.

Aaron looked over at me and asked if Doc had given her some kind of medicine that was making her loopy. This just made her laugh more as I turned looking between my brother and husband.

"Well...Doc gave us both an I.V. since we were both dehydrated. I need to start eating more and I need to drink more fluids. Doc thinks that I was feeling dizzy because of my sugar was low...so he is going to keep an eye on me. Alyssa is fine she just needs to eat healthy and drink fluids too. Let's see what else. Oh...Doc gave us both vitamins to take and he said if mine didn't help me gain some weight he would switch them."

Jayce looked at me confused as he asked, "Angel why does Doc think you need to gain weight...is there something wrong with you?"

I just looked at Jayce and Aaron and then over at Alyssa; as she sat still laughing.

I looked between my brother and husband as I took a deep breath, then told them both.

"Well...uh...there kind of is something. It turns out that Alyssa and I both are six weeks pregnant."

Jayce and Aaron just sat there looking from me to Alyssa stunned for a moment before both of them started grinning.

I cleared my throat to get their attention.

"Also…I forgot to tell you it seems we are both due in July."

Aaron and Jayce both started laughing…

This only caused Alyssa to laugh harder almost falling off the couch.

I just sat there and looked at all three of them wondering if maybe they had all lost their minds.

I got up off the couch to leave them to their craziness…

Before I could make three steps Jayce dropped to his knees as he placed his hand on my stomach. He looked up at me smiling as pure happiness shown in his eyes.

"Angel, you are having my baby boy. I love you both so much."

I leaned down and kissed him as Aaron picked up Alyssa. She had finally fallen off the couch and was now lying on the floor. He started spinning her round and round, as they both continued laughing.

Later that night…

I was lying in bed waiting for Jayce to finish his shower.

I put my hand on my stomach as I started to daydream about having a family with Jayce.

I never would have expected to be having a baby when I went to see Doc this morning.

It really never crossed my mind since life hadn't seem to slow down enough for me to even think about kids.

Jayce came out the bathroom and crawled into bed next to me. He laid down on the bed pulling me in his arms as he put his hand over mine. We stayed that way together with our hands lying over where our child was now growing as we both fell asleep.

The rest of the week found me feeling much better…

The vitamins were helping me a lot and I was beginning to feel more like me.

We had planned on telling John and Victor on their birthdays as a surprise.

When my father was alive…

We use to fly to Italy to celebrate his, Victor and John's birthday with a big party every year.

Since my father was gone, we decided not to go to Italy this year.

Victor called us and told us he would see us at Christmas instead. It was the first time we didn't celebrate their birthdays together in Italy.

On the morning of Victor's birthday I called to tell him about the baby but made him promise not to tell John. We were waiting until the next day to surprise him for his birthday also.

Nick talked to me after I talked to Uncle Vic to tell me exciting news of his own…

He told me that he and Francesca were expecting a baby also. It was expected to be born in July about the same time as Alyssa's and mine.

I told Jayce the news and he reached for the phone smiling.

He and Nick began arguing over which one would win the bet...

This went on for a good ten minutes or so before he told Francesca congratulations.

Jayce and I went over to Sea Court Manor to tell Marie and John the next day.

I watched as my husband told his father we were having a baby. John smiled and chuckled before telling everyone in the room he was going to be a grandfather.

Aaron told John and Marie that he and Alyssa were expecting too.

Marie started crying and laughing as she told John she would have two babies to spoil.

Uncle John and the others were very surprised when I told them Nick and Francesca were expecting too.

Even without my father and mother there, I could feel how happy they were about the babies.

Aaron smiled at me when I told him that mom and dad would be proud of all of us.

John hugged me telling me he knew our parents were looking down on us–very proud of how we had grown up.

Chapter 10

By the time December's cold winds came blowing thru the towns...

I could no longer fit into my old clothes and Jayce found me crying on the floor of our closet.

He took me into town to buy some maternity clothes and we ended up coming home with more than I could possibly ever wear.

I went to see Doc for my check up and asked him why I was showing so much more than Alyssa. Since, her bump was hardly noticeable at all! He told me with me being so small that I would show much sooner than her but not to worry. He checked me out saying that both baby and I were doing well.

Alyssa's check-up went great too and to celebrate we went to the diner for milkshakes with extra whipped cream and sprinkles.

I was only two and half months pregnant when Rocco's 26th birthday came on December 12th. I was already having some trouble getting up when I sat down and was already begin to not be able to see my own feet.

Alyssa had just started showing good.

Nick had said when I talked to him earlier that day that Francesca had finally started to show also.

I was a little jealous as I hobbled around...

While Alyssa walked around just fine and dandy but I was too happy to care.

Two days later...

Alyssa and I had planned to go Christmas shopping and Lily was supposed to go with us.

That morning I woke up and got dressed. Just as I finished my phone began to ring.

I answered it to find that Alyssa wasn't feeling well and couldn't go shopping with me. I told her it was fine. Lily was going with me so I wouldn't be alone. I told her I would call and check on her later.

I drove to Ravenhall Manor to pick up Lily before we headed into town. Lily had told me she would drive but I told her I was fine driving.

We headed into town and stopped at the shops to pick up all the things we needed on our list. Alyssa had told me what she needed picked up. So, Lily and I went ahead and did her Christmas shopping for her.

We had just finished loading everything in the car when Lily turned grabbing my arm shaking.

I turned to see what was wrong and saw Oscar standing across the street talking to someone, I couldn't see who.

I grabbed Lily and told her to get in the car and drive. I reached for my gun as she opened the driver's door.

Oscar looked up and saw me and started walking toward us.

Just as Lily got my car started and reached to shut her door...

Oscar raised his gun pointing at her thinking it was Alyssa in the car.

I raised my gun and shot him in the throat, not blinking an eye...

Uncle John came round the corner just as I fired the gun. John came running over to me and I told him I was fine. He told me to get in the car and have Lily take me home. He told me to go ahead and leave, he would take care of Oscar.

Lily drove toward Legacy Meadows, as I called Jayce on the phone to tell him what happened. He told me to go straight home and he would be there soon.

After I hung up with Jayce I called Alyssa to check on her.

She told me she was feeling better. I told her about what happened with Oscar. She said she would meet me at my house and wait there with me and Lily–until Jayce or one of the other guys came.

Lily drove my car inside the garage just as Alyssa pulled up. We helped her unload the presents we had picked up for her and put them in her car. Lily left hers in my car until Larson came over to pick her up.

We went inside and sat down in the living room to tell Alyssa everything that had happened that day.

Just as we finished telling her about Oscar the doorbell rang.

I got up to go answer it with my gun in my hand and my finger on the trigger.

I opened the door and had just enough time to shoot...

The bullet hit Troy before he could raise his gun and fire.

Lily was screaming my name as she and Alyssa came running to the front door.

I shot two more rounds into him as Lily and Alyssa came over to stand beside me looking down at Troy's body.

I turned around and told them everything was fine but I needed to call someone.

I picked up my phone and dialed Jayce as Alyssa and Lily stood huddled together shaking.

It only rang once before he picked up.

"Angel did you make it home ok? I just got to the station. I will be home soon. Baby, what's wrong?"

I just stood there shaking with my gun still gripped in my hand...

I put a shaky hand on my stomach, where our child was safe and sound.

"Jayce...you need to come home now. Troy showed up here with a gun but I killed him. I am fine...everyone else is fine too, but I really need you to come home right now."

I could hear my husband yelling to John that Troy showed up at our house.

He told me he was on his way and that Rocco should be here any minute…since he called him right after I told him about Oscar.

I had just hung up the phone when I heard Rocco yelling my name from the driveway as he jumped out of his truck. Before I could walk back over to the door Rocco came running in the house.

As soon as he saw me he pulled me in his arms asking if I was hurt or needed him to call Doc. I told him I was fine and that Troy didn't have time to shoot before I killed him.

Rocco left to go outside on the porch to move Troy's body. I could hear the sound of several trucks speeding toward the house.

I walked outside followed by Lily and Alyssa–both had calmed down since Rocco arrived.

Jayce jumped out of his truck and came running over to me. He checked me over to make sure I wasn't hurt and then kissed me.

Aaron came over to me hugging me close as he asked if I was ok, before going to pull Alyssa in his arms.

Ben and Gage went to help Rocco move Troy's body into back of Rocco's truck. Rocco came over to tell me he was going to get rid of the body before he left.

Jayce told me to take the girls inside while they cleaned the blood off the porch.

Larson walked in to get Lily and I walked with them to the garage to get the presents she had bought. Larson loaded the present in the truck while Lily hugged me and Alyssa good-bye.

Lily still smiled and believed in rainbows...but even I could tell the past year had changed her...along with me in ways we never would have imagined.

After everything was cleaned up Aaron and Alyssa left to go home.

Gage and Ben left shortly after promising to call me later. I waved as they drove away before turning to walk back in the house...while Jayce pulled his truck in the garage.

I closed and locked the front door and headed toward the kitchen.

I had just walked into the kitchen as Jayce was closing the garage door when I felt this strange feeling in my stomach. I took my gun and laid it on the counter and put my hand on my growing belly.

Jayce walked over and asked me what was wrong.

"Jayce I think there is something wrong. I keep feeling this weird fluttering in my stomach. I think you should call Doc," I told him as I stood frozen.

Jayce grabbed the keys he had just hung by the door and came over picking me up in his arms. He put me in his truck and then took off toward town.

As soon as we got to Doc's office he rushed me into a room. Doc checked me over and then told us everything was fine. He said the fluttering I was feeling was the baby moving; and because I was so small, I would most likely feel the baby earlier than most.

We left the office and turned to go back home. I told Jayce that I wanted to get a milkshake and takeout from the diner before we left town.

He just laughed as he turned heading to the diner.

I had drunk more milkshakes since I found I was expecting than I ever had, I believe in my whole life!

Jayce ran in the diner and picked up the food before we left to head to Legacy Meadows.

After we had eaten, Jayce told me to go take a bath while he cleaned up.

When I got out the tub, I got in the bed waiting for Jayce to shower. I had already fallen asleep before he ever made it to bed. Jayce crawled in beside me pulling me in his arms never waking me.

Christmas morning ...

I woke to find the morning sickness had finally stopped!

I told Jayce it was the best Christmas present I could have gotten!

Victor, Buono, Nick and Francesca had flown in from Italy the day before, on Christmas Eve. We were all having Christmas together at Angel Crest Estate. Victor and the others had all spent the night with Stefano.

I woke up feeling very good but also very, very hungry.

I told Jayce I was starving as I looked over at him still lying in bed beside me. Christmas morning was one of the few mornings that Jayce would sleep late.

Jayce offered to make pancakes as he reached over to help me out of bed.

I got dressed as he cooked and then went into the kitchen to eat.

After we finished eating and Jayce was dressed; we loaded the car and left for Angel Crest Estate.

I was excited to see Nick and Francesca since I hadn't seen them since Stefano and Costa's birthday party in October.

Jayce and Nick talk almost every other day, but it not the same as seeing him.

I could see Angel Crest Estate lined with everyone's cars but ours.

"I guess everyone is here but us. It seems like we are late."

He just smiled at me and laughed. Jayce pulled the car around in front of the house parking it over beside Ben's truck. Ben had left just enough room for us to park.

Stefano was waiting with the front door open as Jayce and I got out the car. Stefano yelled for Ben to come help us unload the presents from the car.

Ben came running out the house and helped Jayce lift the presents out the car. I turned to reach to grab one, only to be lifted away from the car by Ben.

I stuck my tongue out at both of them before I turned and left them to get the gifts. I headed up to the house as Stefano stood there laughing at me.

I walked in the living room and Nick walked over pulling me into a hug. He stepped back and looked at me.

"Princess you look beautiful. Look at that little guy, he is just a growing. Princess you are really showing!"

I just looked at Nick in shock, just before I swung and hit him on the arm.

"Niccolò DeLuca, are you calling me fat! I can't believe you."

Nick just shook his head as he looked me with wide eyes.

"No Princess of course not...you look beautiful! I only meant that you are showing more than Francesca and Alyssa...that's all I promise. Arabella you know I love you and I would never call you fat Princess."

I told him it was ok and that I understood what he meant. I explained to Nick that Doc said with me being so small that I would show sooner.

Nick helped me over to the couch as Jayce walked in and started telling them; that I had felt the baby sooner because of my size, too.

Everyone gathered in the living room and we all opened presents...

We all laughed as Ben tried to switch one of his presents with Gage, before Gage punched him.

After the presents were opened, Stefano and the other elders went to the kitchen to check on lunch.

Jayce and the guys were all sitting around talking together on one side of the room. All the girls were over on the couch on the other side talking and laughing too.

Lily was listening to the story about telling the guys we were pregnant...

I was telling Francesca that I had to tell Jayce and my brother since Alyssa wouldn't stop laughing.

Lily turned and looked at Alyssa asking her why she was laughing so much that day.

Alyssa smiled and said, "When Doc said Arabella and I both were having a baby in July...all I could think about was that stupid bet. And then when I found out Francesca was expecting the same time...all I could do was laugh."

I just shook my head at Alyssa before I looked at Lily.

"You should have seen Alyssa that day...all she could do, was just sit there and laugh! I had to tell my husband and my brother that they were both going to be dads. Jayce was excited...but after he found out about Nick and Francesca he was something else. I remember him taking the phone from me and telling Nick he was going to win the bet. I have not heard the end of it since. Just yesterday I was telling Jayce that we needed to think about picking out a girl name too...and just looked at me and told me no. He said we didn't need to because I was having a boy and he would be born on his birthday...along with Aaron and Nick's. He is driving me crazy...but man do I love that man."

I laughed as Alyssa, Francesca and Lily just looked at me laughing as tears ran down their faces.

Stefano called out that lunch was ready as we all walked into the kitchen still laughing.

Nick asked us what was so funny but his wife told him it was just girl stuff.

Lunch was wonderful and the table was filled with food covering from one end to the other.

Stefano had made rigatoni with lamb, meatballs with bruschetta and his famous Christmas pasta.

Costa made spicy marinated olives, Italian stuffed sausages and Italian gnocchi with pomodoro sauce. It was a feast...

Everyone ate and talked until late in the afternoon before Jayce loaded our gifts in the car and we headed back to Legacy Meadows. I leaned back in the car as he drove drifting off as the radio played with Jayce singing along.

New Year's Eve...

We all celebrated the New Year come in together at the diner with milkshakes and burgers with fries.

Ben drank more milkshakes that night then all of us! Jayce told him he was going to be sick but Ben just kept drinking them one after another.

That night we left the diner around one and ended up back at Legacy Meadows...

All of us camped out in my living room.

The guys laid sleeping bags on the floor surrounding the couches. Lily, Alyssa and I each chose a couch for our bed with each of our husbands lying beside us on the floor.

We all stayed up watching movies until everyone fell asleep around four.

Ben and Gage insisted we have popcorn, drinks and candy snacks. Gage said it was the only way to watch a movie. Ben agreed and pouted until I gave in and said yes.

I don't even know how the guys ate it all, considering they had each ate at least two burgers each at the diner.

John and the others had left the diner and went home for the night telling us they were too old to stay up any later.

Lily, Alyssa and I fell asleep shortly after the movie started since the three of us were so tired.

The next morning...

I woke up to my phone ringing and reached over to answer it before it woke everyone. I picked up the phone getting off the couch and walking to the kitchen before answering it.

"Good morning Princess...I am sorry for calling so early but I wanted to tell you I have to leave town. Victor is sending one of his planes to pick me up and it should be here soon. I have to go out of town to take care of some urgent business, but I wanted to talk to you before I left. It is nothing for you to worry about I just need to take care of a few things. I hope to be back in a week or two but I will try to call again as soon as I can. I love you Arabella and I will see you soon. You take care of yourself and the baby," Costa told me as I stood in the kitchen.

I ask Costa where he was going...

He wouldn't tell me no matter how many different ways I asked him.

I finally gave up and told him to be careful. He promised to call me when he could.

I had just told him I loved him and hung up the phone when Jayce came walking in the kitchen.

Jayce asked me who had called and I told him what Costa had said.

I asked my husband if he knew what was going on and he told me he didn't. Rocco walked in the kitchen as I was explaining to Jayce what Uncle Costa had told me...

But he didn't know anything either.

Before long everyone was awake so we all left to go to Gino's for lunch.

Jayce had called John before we left the house, to ask about Costa but he just told him it was nothing for us to worry about.

We didn't hear anything from Uncle Costa as a week and a half came and went.

I was really starting to worry...

Especially since every time I called I could never reach Uncle Costa and I called every day.

I had an appointment with Doc for a checkup on January 12th that my husband had scheduled the day before; since all I could do was worry about Uncle Costa.

I woke up the morning of the appointment to feel the baby moving. I yelled for Jayce as I was lying in bed with my hand on my stomach talking to the baby.

Jayce came running in the bedroom to see what was wrong. I looked up at him and told him I could feel the baby moving all around. He smiled at me as he came to help me up and told me to get ready while he finished cooking breakfast.

When we got to Doc's he checked me and said everything was going along just fine.

I told him I could feel the baby just moving around.

Doc said he wasn't surprised as small as I was and as active as the baby was.

Jayce stopped by the diner to pick me up a milkshake before we headed back home to Legacy Meadows.

Rocco called while we were on the way home to tell Jayce he had the new vendor list for him. Jayce told him to meet us at the house.

I could see Rocco sitting on the front porch as we pulled in the drive. Rocco came over to the truck to help me out and I started telling him about how I could feel the baby moving.

I left Jayce and Rocco talking on the front porch and walked in the house.

I had just walked in the kitchen when I noticed the light blinking on the machine. I went over and pushed the button to start the message.

"Hello Princess...I wanted to let you know that Costa Accardo is dead. He lasted longer than I thought...but he still did not give up where you are. It was so lucky he had your home number in his phone so I could call you personally...it's just too bad that husband of yours doesn't have this number listed. But I will still find you...and you will give me what I want or I will kill you and your baby. I will see you very soon Princess."

I started screaming when the message ended.

Jayce and Rocco came running in the house with their guns drawn.

Rocco and Jayce found me on the floor crying and screaming...

Jayce came running over to me putting his arms around me.

Rocco asked me what was wrong as Jayce tried to get me to calm down.

I just pointed to the machine as I held on to my husband's arms...trying to keep from shattering as I sat shaking and crying on the floor.

Just as Rocco pushed play the man's voice began to fill the kitchen as I listened to the message play again. I just sat on the floor crying as Jayce looked over at Rocco as the message played.

As soon as the message ended:

Jayce told Rocco to call Stefano and John as he picked me up in his arms and carried me to the couch.

Jayce wrapped me in a blanket as I sat rocking back and forth crying.

I could hear Rocco in the kitchen on the phone talking.

Jayce sat with me curled into his side holding me tightly as he called his brother and mine. It wasn't long before the front door flew opened and Aaron and Ben came running in the living room.

Aaron came over to me and wiped the tears from my face as he pulled me close. I sat there listening to Aaron's heartbeat as I shook and cried in his arms.

Before long my living room was full with everyone in our family trying to find out information.

Alyssa tried to get me to drink something but I didn't want anything.

Jayce picked me up and carried me to bed as he tucked me under the covers. He kissed me and told me to try to get some sleep.

I woke up around one and stumbled back in the living room.

Lily made me a sandwich and she and Alyssa sat with me while I ate.

Jayce and the others were still on the phones...

Rocco came over to sit by me telling me Victor was on his way. Rocco sat back on the couch pulling me close so that my head was lying on his shoulder.

Lily had turned the TV on and was trying to distract me with a movie.

Ben had left the house around four and ran to the diner for food for everyone at the house.

Ben walked over to sit beside me smiling, "Arabella, I got you a burger and fries and I got you a milkshake, with extra cream and sprinkles."

When I told him I wasn't hungry he looked at me worried.

"Princess you have to eat...you and I both know that Costa would want you to take care of yourself and the baby."

I tried to smile at him as I took the milkshake and started to drink it not wanting to worry him more. Ben sat beside me until I had eaten all of my food before he took the trash into the kitchen.

I got off the couch and walked in the kitchen where Stefano, John, Benito, Rocco, Larson, Ben, Gage, my husband and my brother were all talking.

I overheard Stefano telling them, "...he is sure it was for Costa. Victor sent one of his men to get him..."

I was filled with relief that he was alive!

I started to speak getting everyone's attention as they all stop talking and turned around facing me.

"He's alive...Uncle Vic found him? Let's go...we'll take the plane and go get him. Uncle Stefano you know where he is right? Why are you all just standing there...let's go now!"

I demanded as they just stood still looking at me with concerned and worried faces.

John walked over to where I was and told me to sit down.

I told him I didn't want to sit down as he looked at me.

"Arabella, Costa is dead. Princess...one of Victor's men is going to get his body. Do you understand love?"

Stefano walked over and took me by the hand leading me to the table.

I felt like I couldn't breathe...

It seemed like everything was crashing down around me.

I couldn't understand why this was happening.

I watched my father killed by White Feather and it didn't hit me like this.

I didn't know who this was or what they wanted from me.

It wasn't just me anymore...

I had to protect my baby.

Just the thought of my baby being hurt began to make me angry and I started to shake as I placed my hand on my belly cradling my child.

I asked them who the man was and what he wanted from me.

Nobody knew what the man thought I had; they didn't even know who he was or least that's what they were telling me.

When I ask John and Stefano where Uncle Costa had gone, neither would answer me.

I got angry that no one would tell me anything and stood up from my chair and started yelling.

"Somebody needs to tell me what the hell is going on right now! Why did Uncle Costa leave to go out of town? I know one of you knows what kind of urgent business he had to take care of. Who killed him and what the hell do they want from me?"

John tried to calm me down telling me that I was safe and that all this yelling wasn't good for the baby.

That only made me madder as I started yelling again louder.

"You know what's not good for the baby? I will tell you what's not good for the baby. Me...not knowing what the hell is going on, that's what!"

Just as I finished I heard a voice that stopped me dead in my tracks.

"That is quite enough Arabella. I know you are upset and I promise you I will tell you everything I can, but you have to stop yelling. All this stress is not good for you or the baby. You either calm down now...or I will have Doc come give you something to calm you down," said Victor standing behind me.

I just turned and looked at Victor not quite believing he was actually standing in front of me...

I began to start shaking and broke down crying as the room began to spin. I could feel the ground beneath me seem to disappear as I tried to stand.

Nick ran over and grabbed me pulling me in a hug trying to keep me from falling; while he yelled for someone to call Doc.

I shook my head trying to bring the room into focus as I felt my knees start to buckle. I held on to Nick to keep from falling to the floor as I told them I would be fine but no one would listen to me.

Ben grabbed the phone calling Doc to tell him what was happening.

I could hear him telling Doc, that I was shaking so bad that Nick was holding me up to keep me from falling to the floor.

Ben hung up the phone telling everyone that Doc was on his way. He told Jayce that Doc had said to keep me warm and get me off my feet before I fell.

Ben told Nick that they had to try to get me to calm down before the baby went into distress...or my blood pressure dropped too low harming me or the baby.

Jayce and Nick both held me up as they lead me to the living room and sat me down on the couch.

Jayce reached on the back of the couch for the blanket wrapping it around me as he held me close to his chest.

I could hear Alyssa's panic, as she asked my brother what was going on.

It didn't take Doc long to get to Legacy Meadows. After he had checked me he told the others I was in shock. He gave me a shot that he told me would make me sleep.

I could hear him tell me that everything would be ok...just before I felt my eyes closing. Jayce picked me up in his arms and carried me to bed tucking the covers around me before kissing my forehead.

The next morning I woke up to find Jayce still sleeping beside me. I didn't want to wake him so I slipped out of bed.

I was hoping yesterday was a bad dream but I knew that Uncle Costa was gone. Not wanting to face anyone yet I went to the bathroom and took a long bath.

When I knew I could no longer put off facing the real world. I got out of the tub and got dressed.

I could hear Jayce and Nick talking as I left the bedroom and walked in the kitchen.

I told them good morning as they turned around smiling at me.

Nick asked how I was and I told them I was hungry.

Jayce told me to sit down as he grabbed a bottle of juice from the fridge and handed it to me before starting to cook breakfast. I sat down and opened my juice drinking a big sip before sitting it down on the table.

At the smell of food Ben and Gage came walking in the kitchen. They both ask me if I was ok, sitting down at the table next to me.

Nick helped Jayce cook breakfast while we sat around talking. Just before the food was finished Aaron and Alysaa came in the kitchen. Alyssa sat while Aaron when to help Nick and Jayce finishing up and bring the food to the table.

When everyone had sat down and we started plating the food, Lily and Larson came in joining us at the table.

After everyone was finished eating we were sitting around talking when the doorbell rang. Ben told us he would answer it as he ran to the front door.

It wasn't long before I heard the front door close and Ben came walking in the kitchen with a long white flower box. He walked over handing it to me.

"Arabella this just came for you. It looks like you got flowers."

I took the box as I looked at my husband smiling and told him, "Jayce you got me flowers! That's so sweet, thank you."

Jayce just looked at me and shook his head saying that he didn't order the flowers.

I looked around the room waiting for someone to tell me they had sent them to me but everyone shook their heads.

I lifted the lid off the box and handed it to Ben. I pulled back the paper and saw black roses tied with a purple ribbon.

There was a card lying on top of the roses and I reached in to pick it up before I opened the card.

Inside the card read:

My Condolences, Arabella

See you soon.

I looked up at Jayce as I handed him the card. I couldn't stop shaking as I realized who it was from.

Everyone else was talking trying to figure out who had sent the roses.

"He knows where we live Jayce. He has found me and now he is coming!"

I told them as I began to panic.

Jayce looked at me and I could see the anger brewing in his eyes.

"He won't touch you Angel. You and our baby are safe...I promise. Please try and stay calm," he pleaded with me.

Aaron was already on the phone calling John and Nick was on his phone calling Victor. I could hear Victor yelling over the phone as he told Nick he and Buono would be here soon.

I just sat in my chair, I couldn't move as Ben lifted the box taking it off the table.

Alyssa and Lily sat listening as the guys argued back and forth about what we should do. I looked over at Lily to see she was looking at me with fear and concern.

Victor and Buono walked in the house several minutes later and everyone stopped talking.

Victor asked where the box was and walked over to look inside–after Jayce had pointed to where Ben had put it.

Buono came over to me and bent down by my chair. He looked at me and asked me if I was doing ok.

I just looked at him and nodded as John and the others came walking in the kitchen.

Buono helped me up out of my chair and walked me into the living room leading me over to the couch.

Alyssa and Lily followed behind us and sat on the couch with me.

Buono told us to stay on the couch before he turned to Alyssa, "Keep an eye on Arabella. Try to talk to her and keep her calm. Yell if you need anything. I will be in the kitchen with Victor."

He reached for my hand as he bent down to look in my eyes.

"Arabella...you need to try to stay calm so your blood pressure doesn't drop like yesterday. Nobody is going to hurt you or the baby, you have my word. We will find whoever is doing this and I will make sure they are taken care of."

He squeezed my hand before standing and walking back in the room with the others.

Alyssa turned on the TV trying to get me interested in a movie she had found. It wasn't long before the three of us were huddled together completely focused on the TV.

Sometime later just as the movie was ending, Ben came in and told us we were going to town to eat.

Everyone loaded in the cars and we headed to Cardea Steakhouse. No one said a word about the flowers or Uncle Costa as we all sat eating and talking.

When Jayce and I got in the car to go back home I asked him what was going on. He told me that Victor had called his men and they were searching for the man that sent the roses and to try not to worry.

Two days later...

We buried Uncle Costa on the hill overlooking the vineyards of Angel Paradise.

Stefano had picked out a beautiful tombstone with angel wings carved beneath his name along with a lovely Italian prayer engraved in the stone.

Victor, Nick and Buono left to go back to Italy the next morning. Victor tried to get Stefano to go with them but he didn't want to leave Angel Crest Estate or Costa.

On the morning of the funeral Victor received a call from one of his men telling him the problem had been taken care of.

When I asked him who it was that killed Costa and why, he only answered, "Arabella, he is dead my men took care of him. It's over now. No one is coming after you. I promise love...you are both safe."

He never would tell me who the man was, but I suspected it wouldn't be long before I found out the truth.

I told Jayce later that night that eventually all the secrets that Victor, John and Stefano were keeping would come out. I just hoped when they did it would explain why the elders acted so odd.

The rest of January was uneventful as life returned to normal. The baby continued to grow along with my belly. The winery was still doing well as several new vendors joined our family business.

Francesca and the baby were doing well and we talked on the phone now every week.

The only unexpected surprise we had come the last day of the month when Lily showed up on my front porch.

I had just gotten back from town where I had met Jayce for lunch to find Lily sitting on my front porch smiling.

She had just left Doc's and had come over to tell me she was expecting in October. She was so excited and insisted I go shopping with her soon.

We all went out to celebrate that night at Cardea Steakhouse and afterwards stopped by the diner for milkshakes.

Larson told Lily that if she drank as many milkshakes as me that their baby would be born diabetic.

I told him to hush that it wasn't so; because Jayce had already asked Doc about it.

Ben laughed as he listened to Jayce tell them he was worried about the baby with all the milkshakes I had been drinking, so he talked to Doc.

Jayce told them that Doc had laughed at him as he told him the baby would be fine no matter how many milkshakes I drank a day.

Alyssa laughed when I told her that I kissed Doc on the cheek; after he said I could have as many milkshakes as I wanted.

Chapter 11

On the first morning of February I woke up to find it had snowed the night before. It wasn't much just enough to cover the ground and would be melted by late that afternoon when the sun started shining.

I was getting ready to drive into town when I saw snow covering every inch of Legacy Meadows.

Jayce had overslept and walked out the door behind me to go to work when he noticed the snow.

He looked at me and smiled as he told me, "Snow day Angel. I'm not going to work today and you and I are going to spend the day with hot chocolate and movies in bed."

I just turned and looked as his smiling face as he looked across the yard at the white flakes that covered every corner.

I laughed as he stuck his tongue out trying to catch some snowflakes that were still falling from above us.

We turned to go back in the house as Jayce's phone started ringing. My brother had called to tell him he was taking a snow day too, and would call the others and tell them to take the day off.

After I had changed into a pair of warm pajamas I made hot chocolate while Jayce picked out some movies.

We stayed in bed all day watching movies and drinking cocoa.

Jayce called and had pizza and garlic bread delivered from Gino's.

Just before night had fallen I felt the baby kicking.

I told Jayce the baby was kicking and he put his hand on my belly.

We waited while my husband talked to the baby for several minutes before I felt the baby kick again. The more Jayce talked to my stomach the more the baby would kick.

Lying down next to Jayce I told him I couldn't wait for him to feel our child kicking, just before I fell asleep.

Stefano called the next morning to let me know that Rocco was on his way to pick me up. Carlos had call Rocco and told him that Stefano needed to see me at Angel Crest Manor.

I got ready and was waiting when Rocco pulled in front of the house. I closed and locked the front door and Rocco helped me climb in the truck.

We talked about the snow the day before as he drove us to Angel Crest Manor.

Stefano was waiting with Carlos as we pulled in the drive.

Carlos had not left Stefano's side since Uncle Costa was killed. I know Carlos felt responsible for Costa's death but Stefano had told him several times since Costa died he was not to blame.

I stepped out the door as Carlos reached for my hand. He led me over to Stefano as Rocco turned to leave heading back to Paradise Falls. I smiled at Uncle Stefano as he opened his arms for a hug.

After we had sat down in the living room Carlos left to get drinks for us.

I waited as Stefano opened two folders taking out several papers and laying them side by side.

"Arabella...as you know you are heir to Costa's estate and these are the papers you have to sign. Costa had a life insurance just like your parents and the rest of us. It was for $100 million and has already been placed in your account. Costa owned twenty percent of Nostra Tesorino Winery in Italy and twenty percent of the one here which now belongs to you. You also own Angels Paradise consisting of the vineyards, town, and airstrip with the plane hangar along with half of Angel Crest Estate. Now these papers here are for my estate. I have decided since you will be taking over for Costa that I will be stepping down. I would like for you to take over for me now as well. Princess you are ready...and the boys will help you. I will still stay here at Angel Crest the only thing that will change...is that you will take over the business."

I just looked at him as I tried to breathe thru the shock.

I knew this was coming...

Uncle Stefano hadn't been the same since Uncle Costa died.

I knew the money had already been put in my account.

My father set up an account for me and Aaron for when he died.

My father and mother both had a $100 million life insurance over both of them which Aaron and I received. We each got half of the $200 million insurance policy, but Aaron had gotten my father's entire estate.

He had set it up that way, not leaving me anything but the insurance because I was heir to Uncle Costa and Stefano.

I didn't care about getting Haven Falls; I truly thought it was fine since the elders had agreed.

I looked at him and nodded to continue as I signed the papers for Uncle Costa's estate. After I had finished signing the last paper he reached for his and began to talk.

"These papers are my estate and life insurance. My life insurance of $100 million will be placed in your account on my death. But for now, everything else will be transferred to you as of today along with Costa's estate. You now own Angels Falls consisting of the vineyards, town, and winery buildings and office. Twenty percent of Nostra Tesorino Winery in Italy and twenty percent of the winery here that was in my name is now yours. Mine and Costa's together give you forty percent ownership of Nostra Tesorino Winery in Italy and forty percent in America. You now have controlling interest in a multi-million dollar winery, Princess."

I wasn't sure what would happen now…

If Stefano and Costa had this much faith in me, I wasn't going to let them down.

After I had signed all the paper we sat with Carlos talking. I may now own Stefano's estate but he had set aside some for Carlos. Carlos already had money, since he received his father's life insurance when he died.

Stefano warned me that the other two clans could have problems with me taking over but not to worry–they had a plan.

Jayce came and picked me up later that afternoon to go back to Paradise Falls. My husband told me that everything would be fine when I asked about the other two clans. He said that Victor and the others had a plan...if the other clans said anything or tried to cause a problem.

We stopped by the diner and ate before heading home to Legacy Meadows.

The next night after Jayce came home from work Victor called. I asked my husband what was wrong, but he only told me not to worry.

I just wished all of them could understand...

When they tell me "not to worry" it only makes me worry that much more! Yet they all do it, all the time.

I wish they would just tell me what's going on, instead of trying to keep things from me. I am going to find out anyway.

The next morning I woke up to find my husband still in bed asleep next to me.

I knew that the phone call from Victor last night was something to worry about...

But I knew Jayce would tell me when he was ready.

I got up and went in the kitchen to find something to eat.

Jayce walked up behind me just as I closed the fridge. He leaned down kissing me on the shoulder.

"Angel, I am taking some time off from work and spend it with you. Things have been so crazy lately with what happened to Costa...I think we need a vacation. Beside you have a doctor's appointment on the 12th for the ultrasound and I want to be there. So what do think? Hey...we can decorate the nursery!"

I knew this sudden vacation had to do with Victor's call but I really wanted to decorate the nursery. I told him I would love to fix the nursery and a vacation sounded great.

We ate breakfast and got ready to go shopping.

We went into town and found everything we needed for the nursery.

Jayce picked up four different little boy outfits but refused to let me get any little girl clothes! Every time I picked up anything that was pink; Jayce would shake his head before taking it and putting it back.

It was late when we finished shopping and since everything was being delivered the next day, we went out to eat.

We went to Cardea Steakhouse, to meet up with Ben and the others.

Alyssa and Lily asked me about the nursery and we spent the meal looking at pictures of what we had bought.

Alyssa told Aaron that he needed to take off and take her shopping too. Aaron promised to take her the next day as the waiter brought our food to the table.

Whenever we went to Cardea Steakhouse; Jayce and the guys always order the 22 ounce porterhouse with truffle fries. The girls and I always order the 12 ounce filet mignon with truffle fries too.

This time I told Jayce I wanted what he was having because I was starving.

Alyssa orders the same thing I do, but Lily just looked at us like we were crazy as she got her usual.

I almost cleaned my plate but there were no leftovers since Jayce finished the rest.

That night when I crawled in bed I fell asleep time as my head hit the pillow.

The nursery furniture was delivered late in the afternoon and my husband was going to put it together himself the next day.

It took Jayce six days to finish putting everything together and finish the nursery. He had insisted on painting the room blue before he would even touch the furniture.

I asked him what he was going to do if Doc said it was a girl.

He told me it was a boy and that there was no need to wait for Doc to tell him what he already knew. All I could do was shake my head and laugh as we finished the nursery; so it was ready for our little one.

The morning of my appointment I woke up before Jayce and eased out of bed trying not to wake him.

Valentine's Day was in two days and with my husband home, I hadn't been able to make his card.

I had made Jayce a homemade Valentine's card ever since we were little. It was a tradition and I hadn't been able to sneak away to make it since Jayce had not let me out of his sight.

Whatever Victor had told Jayce and the others had all of them on high alert! Jayce was acting like there was someone around every corner, waiting to take a shot at me.

Stefano hadn't left Angel Crest Estate except once since Victor called Jayce and Carlos had not left his side.

I had just finished the card and hid it behind a book in the office when the phone started ringing.

I heard Jayce answering the phone as I headed back to the bedroom. I found Jayce sitting up in bed talking on the phone; so I crawled up the bed and sat facing him.

I could tell something was wrong because I could see that my husband was getting angry.

I waited until he hung up.

"Jayce...I have been very patient and I haven't asked any question. I have loved having you home but I know something is going on since you have not left my side. You need to tell me what is going on."

Jayce looked at me and I could tell he was trying to figure out how to tell me.

He took my hand pulling me close as he said, "Angel, I don't want you to worry. I need you to stay calm and think about the baby. We have to go your appointment in an hour, but I promise I will tell you everything when we get home."

See...there he goes again with the not worrying! I knew there was no getting anything from him as I got up to go get dressed to leave for town.

When we got to Doc's office…

I crawled up on the table as my husband stood beside me. After Doc had checked me he began the ultrasound, as I turned to look at our baby.

On the screen I could see our baby touching his nose with his hand. I watched as he moved; as Doc told us it was a boy. I had never seen anything so wonderful. Doc said that everything was on schedule just as he started to kick.

I grabbed Jayce's hand putting on my belly as his eyes grew wide, as he felt his son kick against his hand. I was laughing as he asked the baby if he wanted a milkshake and he kicked Jayce's hand.

Doc just looked at my husband with a straight face and told him that meant yes, as I just nodded my head along with Doc.

Aaron and Alyssa had an appointment just before us and were waiting for us in the waiting room.

I walked over to Alyssa and told her we were having a boy and she told me they were too.

Aaron and my brother decided we should go out to celebrate the news so we headed over to Julianna's Diner.

Later that afternoon we headed back to Legacy Meadows and I knew whatever Jayce had to tell me was bad. Aaron and my husband both acted like bodyguards over me at the diner.

Alyssa and I both knew something was wrong but they wouldn't tell either of us a thing. Every time we asked they just changed the subject.

When we got home Jayce took me in the living room and sat down with me on the couch.

"Angel, I love you and I will protect you and our son no matter what. I will tell you what is going on but you have to stay calm."

I nodded my head and waited as he shifted so he was facing me.

"You know that Victor called last week and he called again this morning. When he called last week he told me that Costa death was a hit. Someone placed a hit on Costa and has now put out a hit on Stefano. When Costa was killed two of Victor's men were with him. One was killed along with Costa and the other was injured, before he killed the hit-man. We didn't know there was a hit on Costa until it was too late. Now there is one on Stefano and Victor thinks it's the same person. He is not sure who exactly…but he thinks it's someone in the Camorra Clan. He believes whoever ordered the hit sent you the roses. Since Costa is dead and you are heir to his estate, the other clans have some questions. They do not know that you have taken over for Stefano and Victor is not sure what will happen when they find out. But now that they know you are heir, Alberto Zambrano is demanding a meeting now instead of waiting. We have to leave on Valentine's Day to head to Italy and meet Victor."

I knew this was really bad…

They have never moved a meeting before. I don't think it's ever been moved, for any reason!

It has always been on Venerdi Santo, Good Friday, for generations.

I knew Stefano thought they may have a problem with me, but I never thought they would move the Mafia Clan Heads meeting.

Jayce tried to distract me with picking out names for the baby but I was still worried.

Aaron and Alyssa came over later that night because Aaron wanted to talk to Jayce. Alyssa and I sat in the living room trying to watch a movie to keep our minds off what was happening.

I called Stefano the next morning and he told me not to worry that Victor had everything under control. But he wouldn't tell me how.

See what I mean…they keep telling me not to worry!

I packed our suitcases that night as my husband handed me clothes that we needed to wear for the meeting.

Jayce told me that I couldn't let anyone see my gun and I was not to shoot unless he told me.

I hadn't met all the members of the other clans. I only met two from the Rosarno Clan that were now Head of Family. I had met Gerardo and Federigo only once and that was years ago, when we were in Italy visiting Victor.

When I woke up Valentine's Day my husband had surprised me with breakfast in bed. He had gotten me a dozen red roses and was very surprised when I handed him his card I made. He asked me when I was able to make it without him seeing and I told him how I did when he was sleeping.

After we ate breakfast we got dressed and went over to Story Brooke Manor to pick up Aaron. Larson was staying behind with Lily and keeping an eye on Alyssa for Aaron.

Ben and Gage were not going either and neither one was very happy about it. And they both made sure we all knew just how unhappy they were to be left behind.

Victor had said only the Heads of the Family and their protectors could go. Stefano was going since no one knew I had taken over for him.

Rocco was going as protection for Aaron, Jayce and I, since Carlos was going with Stefano. Carlos and Rocco both were my protectors since Victor insisted I be covered when I wasn't with them. Buono was going with Victor and Nick and would protect all of them when I wasn't there with them.

We met Rocco, Carlos and Stefano at the plane as we boarded and headed to Italy. We were flying to Sicily to meet Victor and stay at Tesori Cove Villa for the night. We would leave the next morning and fly to Florence, Italy together for the meeting.

The meeting location is always changed but is always in a neutral territory. I had never been to a meeting and I knew Jayce, Nick and Aaron had only been once. They all went the year before they took over, with our fathers to meet the other clan heads.

Buono and Victor were waiting when we landed and we all headed to Tesori Cove Villa for the night.

Shortly after we ate I left them talking as I went up to bed. I was so tired, all this traveling and stress with worrying while pregnant was wearing me out. I just barely made it into bed before I passed out.

All I wanted to do was sleep and hope I wake up to find this has all been a bad dream. Oh well, a girl can dream.

The next morning I slid my gun in my boot Aaron and Jayce had given me for graduation; before standing and letting my dress fall showing my ever growing belly.

Jayce walked over to help me slide on my new leather jacket over my dress. He had bought it for me for Valentine's Day since I could no longer fit in the other one.

Jayce opened the bedroom door and held my hand as we walked down stairs to meet the others.

Victor told me I couldn't have a gun but I refused to go without one. He made me promise to leave it in my boot unless the baby or I was in danger.

Victor and Stefano promised me no one would dare harm me since I was carrying an heir.

Victor said me being pregnant would be our saving grace…but he and the others wouldn't tell me why when I asked.

We all loaded in the cars and headed to the plane to fly to Florence for the meeting.

I sat back and listened as they all talked about the different agendas on the meeting list. I was going to wait in another room with Rocco and Carlos until it was time for me to join them.

Buono squeezed my hand as he told me not to worry and that everything would work out fine.

I knew Victor and the others had some ace up their sleeve. But, none of them would tell me what it was.

When we arrived in Florence, four cars were waiting to take us to the meeting location. Jayce held my hand as we drove and Nick just winked as he told me they had it covered.

It didn't take us long before we arrived at a large estate and I asked who it belonged to. Victor said the owner was given a substantial amount of money to vacate the house for the meeting to be held.

Jayce helped me out of the car as we headed inside the front door.

Jayce led me to a room just to the right that held two blue chaises and a gold settee. My husband kissed me as he left me with Carlos and Rocco; as he and the others headed toward the end of the hall. Rocco helped me to sit down as Carlos went and shut the door locking it behind him.

I was glad he locked the door but the reasoning behind it was scaring me a little.

I sat on the settee beside Rocco and laid my head on his shoulder. The meeting had been going on for at least an hour and I was getting tired, so I closed my eyes.

I didn't really want to be here but Victor and Stefano said it was necessary.

Victor told Carlos he would text him when they needed them to bring me in the room.

I wasn't looking forward to walking into a room with all the Heads of the Families of the other two clans.

I knew Victor and Stefano thought that one of them had placed the hit on Uncle Costa and now Stefano.

I knew Victor's man had killed the hit-man responsible for Costa death; but the one that ordered it was still very much alive.

They were sure that both hits were ordered from someone in the Camorra Clan.

I was sure who ever it was, was in that room.

There are three separate Mafia Family Clans:

The Sicilian Mafia or Cosa Nostra as Victor likes to call it is my family.

Our fathers decided years ago that they were going to go somewhat legit and started Nostra Tesorino Winery.

We were originally based in Sicily, Italy and now America too.

The Rosarno Mafia Clan is based in Rome and had been dealing in arms and smuggling for years, but is rumored as trying to go legit.

There are five families that make up the Rosarno Clan.

Each with an heir that is now Head of the Family:

Gerardo Bulgarelli (19)

Ciro Di Pasqua (18)

Federigo Franzese (21)

Giacomo Ermacora (18)

Ponzio Milani (22)

The Camorra Mafia Clan is from Naples and is far from legit or possesses any type of moral compass. They are known for smuggling, money laundering and kidnapping. They are not above torturing children to get what they want.

The Camorra is made up of only four families in which they are all related by blood.

Two brothers, Alberto and Donatello Zambrano, along with their cousins, Ermes Tosto and Vinko Sapienti; make up the Camorra clan.

Alberto's oldest son–Albert (19) is head of the family.

Albert's younger brother Epifanio (18) is ruthless and is seriously psychotic.

Donatello's oldest son–Damian (19) is quite charming as well as his younger brother Daniel (17).

Ermes's son Armando (20) and Vinko's son Vinnie (20) along with Albert and Damian, run the Camorra Mafia.

I would meet all of the clan heads as well as their fathers since all of them had attended this meeting.

Victor said usually only the Head of each family and one or two elders for each clan came along with their protectors.

But for some reason, the entire Camorra clan had attended.

I opened my eyes when I heard Carlos's phone beep and looked at him as he nodded his head to Rocco. Carlos smiled at me and started toward the door as Rocco stood giving me his hand helping me stand.

I looked at Rocco not wanting to go in there, as anxiety gripped me and the baby started to kick against my hand.

Rocco just smiled as he looked down at me.

"You will be fine Princess. Just go in there and don't back down to anyone. Just remember not to let them know you have a gun...whatever you do remember not to shoot. You show them who you are, Arabella Marcello Cardea...the true heir of Costa and Stefano's estate. And you love, are the Principessa, so go in there and give them hell."

I stood up and told them I was ready as we headed in the room where the meeting was being held.

It took a lot of convincing to get Victor to let me bring my gun but I refused to leave the house without it.

Victor and the others didn't want anyone in the Camorra or Rosarno clan knowing that I could shoot.

I thought that maybe either Ponzio or Federigo from the Rosarno Clan knew I could shoot...but I wasn't sure.

Aaron was positive that White Feather had no idea I could shoot a gun, since Troy or Oscar didn't know that women weren't allowed to hold a gun in the Mafia.

Victor and the others insisted that I learn but had kept it a secret from the other clans.

There was never anyone left alive after they saw me with a gun, either by my hands or one of the guys.

So somehow, it had been kept a secret all these years and only a select few even knew I could shoot a gun.

Nobody looked over as us as we walked in as they kept talking among themselves.

I overheard Alberto talking to Stefano and I had to keep from laughing at the things he was saying.

"Costa didn't have an heir and I know it is too much for you to run two families Stefano. My son Epifanio is of age and I have the means to buy out Costa's estate. Epifanio would be perfect to take over the business and could be of great value to you Stefano. I know you don't have any children and you will need someone strong to help you."

I could see Epifanio smirking; as he thought his father had Stefano right where he wanted him. I could see why Uncle Vic thought they were behind Uncle Costa's death.

Victor looked up as I walked over and nodded to Stefano that I was in the room. I could see the three tables where each clan sat and I saw Ponzio nod his head at me and smile.

Stefano looked over at Alberto and calmly said, "Alberto that will not be necessary. Costa's estate has already been settled, the new heir has already taken over. As far as my needing help, I am no longer head as my heir has taken over for me as well."

I could see Epifanio looking from Stefano to his father, as he became furious. He begin slamming his hand down on the table and yelling at Stefano.

"What heirs? Neither of you have any children! Who could you possibly have gotten to take over?"

I was surprised Victor or Stefano hadn't shot Epifanio for his disrespect!

Stefano just calmly looked at Victor as Epifanio continued to throw a fit; as he slammed his hand down on the table repeatedly.

I could see everyone in the room was stunned as they all sat waiting to hear Stefano's answer.

Stefano stood up from his seat and turned to me extending his hand for mine. Jayce was sitting beside Stefano with Aaron on his other side. Nick was between Aaron and Victor with Buono standing behind them.

I took Stefano's hand as Carlos and Rocco both stood by me one on each side. Jayce stood giving me his seat so that I was now seated between him and my brother.

Stefano stood behind my chair with his hands on my shoulders as he began to speak.

"This is Arabella Marcello Cardea. She is Carmin Marcello's daughter and Jayce Cardea's wife. She is heir to both mine and Costa's estate."

I watched as my husband and brother both reached for their guns; as the men sitting at the Camorra Clan table began to argue and fight over this news.

I looked over at the table where the Rosarno clan sat; and noticed no one looked the least bit surprised or even angry that I was heir. It was almost as if they already knew.

Alberto and his brother along with their cousins demanded that I couldn't be named heir. They insisted that it had to be a male heir to take over as head of the families.

I just sat there beside Jayce gripping his hand as I saw Carlos and Rocco move closer to me drawing their guns.

Buono had his gun gripped in his hand and I could tell he was having a hard time not shooting Epifanio, at the looks he was sending my way.

He sat staring at me and it was really starting to unnerve me.

Victor called for everyone to quiet down as Vinko's son Vinnie raised his hand getting everyone's attention.

"Before we sit here and argue all day on this matter...I have one question. For generations it has always been either the first born male or a chosen heir that has the qualities necessary to head the family. Stefano I understand you have chosen Arabella as well as Costa...but she cannot lead your families. We all know it is necessary for the head of the family to be able to protect their clan. Women are not allowed to even hold a gun...let alone shoot one. Unless Arabella is willing to step down as heir and give it to a suitable male...my cousin would be willing to take over."

Vinnie finished talking and sat back in his chair looking quite satisfied, thinking he had somehow won.

I could see several of the men in the Rosarno Clan begin to smile as they looked over at Vinnie.

I looked over at the Rosarno Clan table and saw Gerardo and Giacomo whispering to Ponzio, before looking over at me smiling. Gerardo nodded his head at me and looked at my husband...just as Ponzio stood getting everyone's attention.

I looked over at Nick and Buono watching Ponzio to see what he would do.

I was really wishing John and Benito had come I would feel better if they were here. I was glad Ben and Gage hadn't come because I was sure they would have already shot someone by now.

My hand moved across my belly as he began to kick hard feeling my anxiety.

I needed to get my gun from my boot–as my hand started toward my leg, Jayce squeezed my other hand reminding me I couldn't.

Aaron had shifted in his seat so his body was blocking mine from Vinnie and Epifanio's view. I reached over to grab Aaron's hand as I felt Stefano squeeze my shoulders.

Once everyone had turned to Ponzio, he began to address the room.

"Vinnie you are correct that men hold the position as head of the families. This is an unusual situation and I think I have a solution that will resolve this matter. Arabella has already been named heir but she is currently pregnant with an heir. If she would allow for Jayce, Nick and Aaron to handle all business affairs until her son is of age…I believe we can leave her named heir. She would only be heir on paper but would allow the others to handle the estate affairs. When her son turns eighteen…he will take his rightful place as heir. Victor do you believe this will be fair?"

Victor looked over at me and then turned to Ponzio and said, "I believe this will be amendable. I would like a few minutes to talk to Arabella and the others…then I will have an answer for you."

Ponzio sat down as he told Victor that would be fine.

He looked over at me and smiled as Jayce and my brother helped me from my chair. I turned and followed Jayce and the others back to the room I had waited in before.

I wasn't sure what was happening, but I was not giving up heir after I had promised Stefano I would do a good job.

Rocco opened the door as we all walked into the room and then shut it behind him.

Victor was the first to speak.

"Well that went better than I had hoped. Ponzio is giving us a way out without bloodshed. Arabella...I want you to listen to me carefully. We are going to go back in that room and I am going to tell the others that you are handing over the running of the business to the boys. You will still be heir and nothing will change...you will still make all the decisions but we are not going to let the Camorra clan know. You will tell them you agree and will hand over everything to Jayce, Aaron and Nick. I promise you this changes nothing, we only need to let them think it does...because there is no way I will allow Epifanio or his snake of a father anywhere near Nostra Tesorino Winery."

Jayce and Aaron both told me this was the only way and that everything would be fine. Even Nick agreed as he squeezed my hand.

We all headed back in the room, each taking the seat they had just left.

Victor told everyone in the room that he agreed with Ponzio's idea and that I had agreed to hand everything over.

I could see that Epifanio and his father were not happy. Just before Alberto could make any comment...Ponzio spoke.

"Arabella, do you agree to let Jayce, Nick and Aaron take over until your son is of age?"

I knew I was supposed to say yes, but it was killing me to bow down to the Camorra clan.

I looked at my husband and he smiled as he nodded his head for me to answer.

I looked over at Ponzio as I reluctantly told him, "Yes I agree."

Ponzio just nodded at me before telling the rest of the men that the matter was now settled.

It seems that Uncle Costa estate was the last thing on the list for the meeting, as Victor called the meeting to a close.

Jayce stood helping me from my chair as everyone began to stand.

I watched as Epifanio turned pulling his jacket on and noticed a single black rose pinned to his lapel.

He looked over at me, as he put his jacket on noticing that I had seen the rose. He smiled at me as he headed in my direction, as I grabbed for a hand near me.

Rocco leaned over to ask me what was wrong; since it was his hand I had grabbed.

I squeezed Rocco's hand just as Epifanio walked over to stand in front of us. Epifanio nodded his head at Rocco before looking at me.

"Arabella I wanted to introduce myself...I am Epifanio Zambrano and I am pleased to meet you. I can see why Costa and Stefano are so taken with you...you are quite beautiful."

I just held on to Rocco, as he noticed the rose Epifanio was wearing was the same as the ones I received.

I only nodded at Epifanio as Jayce and Aaron told me it was time to leave–as my husband led me away with arm around my waist.

I could see Rocco getting angry and began pulling him with me, since I was still holding his hand. Rocco threw a look at Epifanio, as he turned to follow us from the room.

We walked out of the house and started toward the car as Federigo called out to Nick. Ponzio and Federigo came walking over to where we stood by the car.

Ponzio looked at me and said, "Arabella...I am sorry if you believe that I feel you are not rightful heir. I have no problems with you being heir, as I know you are quite capable. What happened in that room was the only way to keep from bloodshed...and the Camorra clan from getting their hands on Nostra Tesorino Winery. I hope you understand, and I hope you know that I am a friend. Should you ever need me or any member of my clan, please don't hesitate to call."

I told him I understood and there were no hard feelings.

After everyone had said their goodbyes; we all left and headed back to the plane. As soon as we got to the plane, Victor had us board and Rocco took off heading back to Sicily.

Chapter 12

After we got back home from Italy the rest of February went by quite smoothly.

Stefano was doing much better since Uncle Costa's death and had started to leave the house, spending time with John and Benito.

I helped out with the winery but left most of it to Jayce and Aaron, since it didn't take much to wipe me out. At five months pregnant, he was growing so much I was afraid I would run out of room before I made it the last four.

Stefano had decided to fly to Italy and spend some time with Victor. He left the first week of March. He told me that a spending month in Italy in his hometown would do wonders for him.

Lily went to her two month checkup and found out she had miscarried.

Doc told her it wasn't anything she had done wrong, it just wasn't meant to be. She had started bleeding and hurting in her side the day before and blamed herself for not calling Doc sooner.

Alyssa and I spent a lot of time with her and she eventually got to where she was doing much better.

She finally understood that it wasn't meant to be and was looking forward to trying again in a few months.

Larson wanted to wait to give her time to where she was ready before they tried again.

Stefano came back home to Angel Crest the first week of April and I was excited to see him and Carlos. I had called him every week while he was gone to talk to him and Victor.

Carlos would call Rocco once a week to check in while he was in Italy with Stefano.

Two days after Stefano had arrived in Italy, Victor called Jayce and the others to tell them the hit on Stefano had been called off.

I had told Victor and the others when we got on the plane to leave Florence that I had seen Epifanio wearing a black rose on his lapel.

Victor and the others were not happy to learn that Epifanio was the one to place the hits on both Uncle Costa and Stefano.

It is an unspoken rule between the three clans; a hit on one of the Heads of the Family could only be ordered by another Head of Family within the Mafia Clans. Hits were never taken out on women since they could not protect themselves and were seen as non-threatening.

Of course there had been several wives and mothers killed in the crossfire; but women were never targeted by members of the clans.

White Feather had killed dozens of women within the three separate clans but he always pulled the trigger himself never outsourcing outside help.

I am not sure exactly what Victor had Buono do after I told them about Epifanio. But it didn't take long to find out it was him.

Jayce had told me that Albert and Damian had sworn to Victor they didn't order the hits and that they would take care of Epifanio. It seems, Epifanio had ordered the hits without Albert and the others knowing...or at least that is what Albert claimed.

Albert and Damian both swore they would see that Epifanio was punished; but Buono had told Jayce he doubted anything would be done to him. Albert and Damian only wanted to avoid having to answer to the other clans on Epifanio's behavior knowing he had broken one of the Mafia Clan Laws.

Since the hit was called off on Stefano...

Victor and the others decided not to start a war over Epifanio's treachery.

On the morning of April 5th the Mafia Clan Laws were not only broken but shattered...inciting a possible all-out war between the clans.

Jayce had left to go to work and I was in the kitchen making cookies.

I had started craving Julianna's double chocolate cookies with raspberries and Sue couldn't keep enough made-up for me and the customers. So, she had given me the recipe.

Ben was coming over at ten that morning to spend the day with me and I had decided to bake another batch of cookies, knowing he loved them too almost as much as me.

I had just taken the pan from the oven when the timer beeped and laid the pan on the counter to cool.

I was getting a plate for the cookies from the cabinet when the window behind me shattered; as the bullet missing me by inches hit the wine glasses in front of me.

I dropped to floor, as pieces of glass and china came raining down from the cabinet above me.

I crawled across the floor the pieces of glass and china cutting my hands and knees…until I could reach the antique phone that had belonged to my mother.

Aaron had gotten it for me from Haven Manor along with some of my mother's things. I kept it in the kitchen on the counter. I reached up pulling the cord until the phone slid off the counter falling to the floor.

I called Ben at Grey Crest Manor and he answered after only two rings.

"Arabella, I am almost finished with the paperwork. I should be over in about thirty minutes. I hope you saved me some cookies because Sue is sold out at the diner this morning…"

"Ben you need to get over here to Legacy Meadows now…someone just tried to kill me. I'm ok…I wasn't hit, but the bullet came through the kitchen window missing me by inches. I am pretty sure they have a sniper rifle…the shot came from the back of the house."

He told me to stay down and he was on his way.

I knew whoever was shooting had a sniper and I was pretty sure he wouldn't fire again, until I was in his sight. He didn't want to draw attention by shooting multiple times so I stayed down so he couldn't see me.

I knew that the hit-man was waiting and wouldn't leave until I was dead. Hopefully giving the guys time to find him and find out who hired him, before they killed him.

I called Rocco as I waited for Ben and told him what had happened. Rocco was in town at the station talking to John and he told me they were on the way.

I heard Ben open the garage door and looked up as he opened the kitchen door, bending down to crawl over to me. He grabbed a dish towel from the drawer over my head and wrapped my hands trying to stop the bleeding.

Ben helped me crawl from where I was sitting on the floor to the living room before he left to go get more towels. He had just finished pulling the glass shards from my hands and knees when the front door opened; and Gage came over kneeling down beside me.

Gage told Ben that Jayce and the others were behind the house holding the hit-man at gunpoint–after Rocco put a bullet in both his legs.

Ben and Gage helped me stand taking me to Gage's truck before heading to Doc's office. My husband had told Gage to get me to Doc's so he could check on the baby and me.

Ben held the towels against my hands and knees as Gage drove us to town.

Doc said the baby was fine but I had to get a few stitches in my left hand where the glass shards had cut me so deep.

Ben called his brother and told him the baby and I were fine; but I needed stitches in my hand. Jayce had told Ben to take me to Grey Crest and keep me there until they arrived.

I had just sat down on the couch when Alyssa and Lily came running in Ben's living room.

Aaron and the others came in about an hour later telling us the hit-man was dead.

Rocco said he told them that Epifanio had ordered the hit on me–he had offered to pay two hundred and fifty-thousand dollars to have me and the baby killed.

After they had gotten the information from him, my husband put a bullet in his head.

John was on the phone with Victor and I could hear Uncle Vic's yelling coming thru the phone. Uncle John handed me the phone since Victor wanted to talk to me. I assured him I was fine, only a few stitches. Victor promised me that Epifanio would pay for trying to kill me.

Stefano had called Ponzio and told him about Epifanio ordering the hit on me–both clans were getting ready for war against the Camorras.

Federigo had told Stefano, "We let the hit he called on you go without punishment, since Albert swore to take care of it. It is one thing to order a hit on you, but ordering a hit on Arabella goes against every law we have. By Epifanio trying to have Arabella and her son killed…he has just signed his death warrant. Alberto can't protect his son this time…"

He and Ponzio were leaving to meet with Victor and Buono to fly to Naples. Ponzio told Jayce he would personally kill Epifanio himself, after he cut off his right hand and would call as soon as it was done.

I stayed at Grey Crest with Alyssa and Lily while Jayce and the others cleaned up at Legacy Meadows.

That night Victor called to tell Jayce that Epifanio was dead and that Buono threaten to kill the entire Camorra Clan, if anything happened to me.

I was afraid that the Camorra Clan would retaliate before long for Epifanio's death. But Jayce told me that Ponzio was keeping an eye on them.

Alberto couldn't stop his death since his son had broken the law going after me and my child.

The rest of the month when by and we didn't hear anything from the Camorra Clan. We had hoped with Epifanio's death that no more hits would be put out on me.

Ponzio started calling me a week after the shooting to check on me and we had become good friends. Ponzio sent a beautiful vintage wood rocking horse for the baby, which Jayce had put next to the crib in the nursery.

Jayce and I finally had picked a name for the baby and were naming him after my father. We had decided on Carmin Jayce Cardea, but were going to call him CJ for short.

Aaron and Alyssa were naming their son Aaron James Marcello, after Alyssa's father James and were going to call him AJ.

Nick and Francesca decided to name their son Niccolò Victor DeLuca, after Nick and Victor, and they were calling him Nico.

Nick was beyond ecstatic at having a son named after him and Francesca told me he went and bought a gun with Nico's name engraved. Francesca was talking to me on the phone and had me laughing so hard...I had to sit down to keep from falling over.

"Arabella, I have no idea why he is buying a gun for Nico now...he is not even here yet! I told Nick that he was a baby–he didn't need a gun. He just looked at me like I was crazy and said he couldn't kill anyone without a gun. He insisted that Nico would need a gun and it made perfect since to go ahead and get it now...I think he has lost his mind."

I wasn't surprised Nick had already bought a gun for Nico–I was glad my brother and husband hadn't bought one. I told Francesca not to tell Jayce and Aaron because I wanted to keep it a secret for as long as possible.

Of course that was a bust, since Nick called both of them after he picked up the gun from the engravers!

Alyssa and I both told them, they were not allowed to buy our sons a gun until they were old enough to shoot it.

Two weeks later...

Jayce went into town and came back with a sterling silver rattle in the shape of a small gun that had our son's name engraved on the handle.

I just laughed as he called Nick and told him that he had bought CJ a gun he could hold as soon as he was born.

Aaron had bought one for AJ also and had brought it home on the same day.

Nick had Jayce send him one for Nico since he couldn't find one anywhere in Italy. It seems my husband and brother had special ordered the rattles the next day; after Nick told them about the gun. Jayce promised Nick he would order one for Nico and send it to him.

On the morning of my 17th birthday CJ woke me up kicking; to let me know he was hungry. He had started about a month ago and the longer I waited to eat...the harder he kicked. He always would stop after I ate but he was so long it would hurt sometimes when he kicked hard.

Doc said he was going to be tall like his father and he was already so long I could barely breathe sometimes. I told Doc and my husband if he didn't come soon I was going to pop!

I opened my eyes to see Jayce standing at the end of the bed. He had a birthday cake with seventeen lit candles held in his hands along with two forks.

"Happy birthday Angel, I got you a cake and two forks!"

Jayce told me smiling at me as he held up the forks.

I just laughed as I sat up and he came over to sit down on the other side of the bed. After he was beside me, I blew out the candles before I reached for the fork and we begin to eat the cake.

"Thank you for the cake...CJ is hungry this morning. He was kicking me so hard it woke me up. I will be so happy when he finally comes I feel like I'm going to pop. Happy Anniversary...my wonderful husband, I love you."

He leaned over and kissed me as he told me Happy Anniversary and that he loved me...before telling CJ he loved him too.

CJ was kicking and dancing as he heard Jayce talk to him. He always seems to know when we are talking to him now.

I was so glad I was three weeks away from my due date because I could no longer see my feet–let alone walk straight!

Doc had said that Alyssa and I both were due on July 1st. But, Jayce and Aaron said their sons would be born on the 2nd or 3rd, depending on which one you ask.

Francesca was not due until July 6th but Nick said Nico would be born early, he was sure.

I wasn't sure what would happen when the babies came.

It seemed no matter when they came someone would be disappointed, I was afraid.

Jayce, Nick and Aaron were so set on this bet about the babies' birthdays…

I had no clue how they would react!

Especially since the closer it got to July, the crazier the guys seem to carry on about this crazy bet.

John and Marie had planned a party for ours and Alyssa and Aaron's anniversary tonight. I told them not to do a party for my birthday this year since it was our first wedding anniversaries.

Jayce and I decided to celebrate my birthday with just the two of us.

After Jayce took the rest of the cake back to kitchen he helped me out of bed. We got dressed to go into town. Since we were going shopping for Lily's birthday present and then having lunch at Gino's for mine.

The party was a success and everyone had a great time.

I missed Victor and Nick but Francesca had been told by the doctor not to fly, until the baby was born. We had all planned to get together after all the babies had been born, so they could meet.

Marie told me that she wished my mom was still here to see how wonderful I had turned out. I told her my mom would love her for how she had taken in me and Aaron.

She had really been a help to me these past few months since I didn't have my mom anymore. I told her not to be surprised if AJ called her *nonna* (grandma) too and she just smiled.

Two weeks later on the morning of Lily's 17th birthday–she called to let me know that the party that night had been changed from the diner to Cardea Steakhouse.

When we left for the party Jayce stopped by Story Brooke Manor to pick up Aaron and Alyssa to ride with us.

When we arrived at the restaurant the parking lot was full of cars. I told my husband it looked like the entire town was here eating.

Lily surprised Alyssa and I with a baby shower and the whole town was there. Lily said that she wanted to share her birthday with me and that we needed a baby shower.

Everyone had brought gifts! Alyssa and I had more clothes than the babies would ever wear.

After everyone had eaten and Alyssa and I had opened all the gifts, I had them bring out a cake for Lily. Everyone sang Happy Birthday and I could tell having everyone accept her meant the world to her.

I think she finally understood she had a family and they all loved her very much.

The phone started ringing at five o'clock in the morning on July 1st waking me and Jayce.

He reached over to answer and I could hear Nick yelling over the phone.

Jayce handed me the phone telling me Nick needed to talk to me and it sounded like an emergency.

I took the phone from Jayce as I tried to sit up before he reached over helping me.

I put the phone to my ear and said hello just before Nick's panic voice came over the phone.

"Arabella...the baby is coming now! What do I do?"

Nick asked me in a panic, as I heard Francesca yell out in pain. I ask Nick if he called the doctor and he told me I was the first person he could think of to call.

I told him to hang up and call the doctor then get Victor and Buono, before he called me back.

He hung up as I started laughing and told Jayce, "Francesca is in labor and Nick is freaking out! He called me instead of calling the doctor or Victor. I don't know what I can do from here but poor Nick is losing his mind."

Jayce just laughed as he took the phone from me and reminded me today was Nick's birthday. He said having Nico born today had probably put poor Nick in shock.

CJ was awake now and kicking so we got up and went to the kitchen to get something to eat.

Nick called back about twenty minutes later to tell me the doctor was on the way and Victor and Buono were with them. I told him to call me back as soon as the baby was born and then I told him happy birthday.

He just laughed and said, "Tell Jayce and Aaron I just won the bet in the best way. Even if CJ or AJ isn't born today...having Nico born on my birthday is the best present I ever got."

I told him I would tell them both and told him to go take care of Francesca.

Jayce started laughing when I told him what Nick had said. We went in the living room and curled up on the couch as we watched movies waiting for Nick to call.

I called Aaron at six o'clock to tell him Francesca was in labor.

Later that morning a little after 7:30 Nick called to say little Nico had just been born. He was a perfectly healthy boy at 7 pounds and 21 inches long. Francesca was doing well. Victor and Buono were fighting over who got to hold him first.

I had never heard Nick sounding so happy in all the years I had known him. Jayce and Nick talked for a few minutes before he hung up looking at me smiling.

Jayce started talking to CJ as he told him all about Nico and how he, AJ and Nico would be best friends.

I laughed as my husband told our son, "Now you stay in mommy tummy today and be a good boy. You can come out tomorrow on daddy's birthday but you have to wait just a little longer."

I asked Jayce to call my brother and let him know that Nick had called, while I called Lily and Larson. We all planned to get together at Gino's for lunch later that day.

Jayce and I drove into town to pick up a few last minutes things before CJ arrived. I wanted to pick up some more diapers and wipes since I wasn't sure we had enough.

After we had finished shopping we met the others for lunch at Gino's.

Jayce reminded me when we finished eating that we needed to stop by the store and pick up a few groceries before we headed home.

Jayce and I loaded the cart before going to check out as I told him, "Jayce we need to stop by the diner and get me a milkshake before we leave town."

He just laughed at me and told me he would get me a milkshake on the way out of town.

We unloaded the car and put everything away before I went to lay down a while. Jayce went into the office while I napped to make a few calls since he needed to return the call he got at lunch.

I woke up and walked down the hall to tell my husband I was awake. He hung up the phone as we walked in the kitchen to start supper.

Jayce had bought steaks and was going to grill them; while I made the salad. After the food was cooked we sat in the living room eating and watching a new movie, we had gotten at the store.

I woke up on Jayce's birthday at four o'clock that morning in labor, as I reached over to wake Jayce. He called Doc and told him the baby was coming; so Doc was on his way to Legacy Meadows.

Carmin Jayce Cardea was born at 6:30 am and was 7 pounds and 21 ½ inches long. He was perfect and I never realized I could love someone so completely.

Doc left after he had checked us both telling Jayce to call him if we needed anything.

Jayce called Aaron and Nick to tell them CJ had arrived. My brother and Alyssa said they were on the way over before hanging up.

By nine that morning everyone was at Legacy Meadows and CJ had been held at least once by everyone there.

Alyssa cried when she saw him and told me she couldn't wait until AJ was born.

Jayce had called Nick to tell him and he said that Nico was doing well.

Ben and Gage went into town late that afternoon and picked up food for everyone and we all sat around eating and talking.

Ben had picked up a birthday cake for Jayce and CJ from the diner. When I told him CJ was too little for cake yet he just shrugged his shoulder–as held CJ showing him his cake.

Aaron had told Alyssa that AJ would be born the next day and she just laughed and said, "You know you might be right especially if he follows his little cousin and Nico. I still can't believe that Nico and CJ were born on their father's birthday."

Jayce just smiled at Alyssa as he told her, their sons were smart and would listen to their fathers when they told them to be born on their birthdays.

Alyssa just looked at me as she shook her head, still not believing the way the bet was unfolding.

I held CJ as I rocked him to sleep that night before I laid him in his bassinet beside our bed.

Aaron called the next morning around eight to tell us AJ had been born at seven that morning. I told my brother Happy Birthday before I handed my husband the phone.

Aaron James Marcello was 7 pounds 9 ounces and was 21 inches long.

Aaron was holding AJ in his arms when we walked in the front door at Story Brooke Manor.

I laid CJ down on the blanket on the floor beside AJ and watched, as Ben and Gage talked to them.

Ben had fell in love with CJ from the first time his brother laid him in his arms.

I knew CJ and AJ would both be beyond spoiled; since the others were already fighting over who would hold them.

Nick and Francesca flew to America a month later and brought Nico for Ben and Gage's 18th birthday party.

AJ and CJ got to meet Nico for the first time.

Victor held CJ in his arms as he looked at Buono and smiled as they both talked to him.

The party was great and Ben and Gage blew out their candles; before Ben came over to take CJ from me to show him the cake. I had to tell Ben not to give CJ any cake, after I saw him trying to feed CJ icing from his fingers.

CJ and AJ were growing bigger every day and they both loved each other.

Alyssa and I made sure to try to get together every day so they could see each other. Alyssa and I would sit and watch as they babbled and cooed at each other and then start to laugh.

Jayce rocks CJ to sleep now every night and calls it their father son time.

I think it is sweet and CJ just smiles and reaches for his father as soon as Jayce comes home from work.

I had to make my husband go back to work after he stayed home the whole month of July and August. It would have been the whole month of September too; if I didn't push him out the door to go to work in the mornings!

On CJ and AJ's 1st Christmas…

Jayce and Aaron opened all the boys' gifts saying they needed help, but Alyssa and I both knew they just wanted to play with the toys…

The four of them played most of the morning along with Ben and Gage until we had to make them stop for lunch.

When January came…

CJ started saying no-no to everything he didn't want to do. I laughed so hard when Jayce told CJ it was time for bath and he just looked at my husband and shook his head and said "no-no, no-no".

CJ was covered in flour from head to toe.

Jayce had unloaded the groceries from the car and sat the bag with flour in it on the floor to shut the door behind him. Before my husband could walk back over to the door to get the bag, CJ had torn it and was playing in the flour.

CJ just looked up at his father and laughed as he threw flour at Jayce. He didn't want to quit playing and take a bath, so he told him "no-no".

It was a sight. I am not sure who was funnier, Jayce or CJ.

Life was good and it seemed like everything was as it should be.

But of course I should have known…

As high as were…

It would come crashing down eventually.

It did come crashing down on the afternoon of February 2nd a little over a year since Costa's death.

I had taken CJ to visit Stefano and Carlos over at Angel Crest Estate. Lily had gone with me since Larson was at work with Jayce and my brother.

Alyssa didn't get to go since AJ was running a little fever and it was too cold to take him out. I promised her I would call her on the way back home, to see if she needed any medicine for AJ.

I had tried to call Alyssa twice on the way back home, but I didn't get an answer.

Just before we got back into Paradise Falls my phone beeped with a message from Alyssa. The message said they were fine and that AJ was sleeping.

I dropped of Lily at Ravenhall Manor, before CJ and I headed home to Legacy Meadows. CJ was just a babbling as he clapped along with the music.

I pulled up in front of the house and saw a package sitting on the front porch.

I pulled the car in the garage and got CJ out the back seat. I walked in the kitchen and put CJ down on the floor to play and went to get the package off the porch. I brought the package in the kitchen and started to open it, as CJ sat on the floor clapping at me.

I opened the lid and froze as I looked inside and saw six black roses along with a note.

I opened the note and read:

Arabella,

Unless you give up heir to me,

I will kill Alyssa along with her son.

I have them both and I will kill them,

unless you sign over heir to me.

-Vinnie-

I started shaking as I reached for the phone dialing my husband and I looked over to where CJ was watching me.

The phone started to ring, just as CJ started crying crawling over to me and I reached down to pick him up.

Jayce answered hearing CJ, "Angel what's wrong? Why is CJ screaming?"

I tried to calm CJ as I held him close as I talked to Jayce.

"You need to come home now and bring everybody! Jayce...please hurry. It's ok CJ...mommy got you. Jayce you need to put Aaron in the truck with you...do not let him drive!"

I held CJ as I tried to assure him I was ok. I knew he was crying because he could tell I was upset and scared.

Jayce didn't ask any more questions; as I hung up and took CJ into the living room trying to calm him down.

It didn't take long before my front door opened and everyone came pouring in. Ben came over and took CJ from me. I knew Ben and Gage would keep him occupied.

I walked back in the kitchen just as Lily came in the front door. My husband looked over and asked me if CJ was ok and I told him he was with Ben.

John had called Stefano and he was on his way.

I told Jayce we needed to call Ponzio and let him know Vinnie was in town...

Then I told them about the roses and Alyssa and AJ.

Victor called Aaron to let him know they were coming and that we would find Alyssa and AJ.

I tried to think of something to do, as I look at Aaron and felt the guilt eating me alive.

"Aaron this is my fault. If I wasn't heir Vinnie would have never taken Alyssa and AJ."

Aaron put his hands on my shoulders and looked me in the eyes–as he told me it was not my fault at all. He made me promise that I understood it wasn't my fault and I had done nothing wrong.

John and the others searched all the towns and couldn't find Vinnie anywhere.

I could tell Aaron was barely holding on as night fell and still no sign of Alyssa and AJ.

I left everyone in the living room as I took CJ to the nursery to rock him to sleep. After he fell asleep, I laid him in the crib and started out of the nursery, as my phone rang in my pocket.

I stepped in the hall to answer it.

"Hello Arabella. I have Alyssa and AJ with me here behind Haven Manor. You need to come alone or I will kill them both now. If I see your husband or anyone else they are dead. Do you understand?"

Vinnie asked me as I heard AJ screaming in the background.

I told him I was coming and not to touch my nephew, or he was dead.

He just laughed, "Not if you come alone, I won't be."

I looked back at my sleeping son before I walked over to my bedroom for my guns. I slipped one behind my back and the other in my boot, before I grabbed the keys to my car.

Everyone was in the living room talking and didn't hear me sneak out the kitchen. I got in my car and eased it out of the garage, as I headed toward Haven Manor.

I looked at the clock on the dash, it read 10pm. I knew Victor and Buono would arrive at Legacy Meadows in about forty-five minutes. I had to hurry because when Victor got there, everyone would know I had left.

I pulled in to Haven Falls just as my phone started ringing. I turned on the road heading to Haven Manor as I pushed the button to answer the call. As soon as the phone picked up I heard Victor's voice come booming over the line.

"Arabella, where are you?"

I looked out the window as I sped toward Haven Manor.

"Uncle Vic, I am almost to Haven Manor."

He asked me why I was at Haven Manor and I told him about the phone call from Vinnie. He started yelling at me to turn around and come back.

I told him I was not coming back without Alyssa and AJ…as I pulled behind Haven Manor and parked.

I told Uncle Vic I had to go and hung up; as I crawled out the car and walked behind the house.

I walked toward the vineyards behind my parents' home until I could see Alyssa holding AJ crying in her arms.

Vinnie was holding a gun to my nephew's head and all I could see was red.

I waited until he stepped over to the side and looked behind me for Jayce and the others. When he was satisfied I had come alone he lowered the gun and stepped away from Alyssa.

I reached for Alyssa and pulled her and AJ behind me as Vinnie just looked at me.

He began to tell me why he should be heir and not me as I reached behind my back.

I waited until he turned looking at the vineyards…as he carried on telling me how all of it would be his, before I slid the gun in my hand.

Just as he turned around to face us, I pulled the trigger and shot him in the throat. I waited until he fell to the ground before I turned around pulling Alyssa and AJ in my arms.

AJ was reaching for me, as I told him it was all over and the bad man was dead.

I reached for Alyssa's hand as I walked them both to my car.

Alyssa crawled in the front seat and I handed her AJ to hold. I got in the driver's side and started toward home.

I called my husband and my brother, to tell him I had Alyssa and AJ and we were on the way back. Jayce and Aaron met us as I came into Paradise Falls. Aaron got in the car with me holding AJ tightly. Jayce followed us home, as we all head back to Legacy Meadows.

Victor and the others had gone to Haven Manor to move Vinnie's body.

Aaron took Alyssa and AJ home, after Victor and the others came back from Haven Manor.

To say I yelled at was an understatement!!

Victor yelled, until Alyssa turned on him and starting yelling back.

"Victor if Arabella hadn't come alone Vinnie would have killed me and AJ! Now stop yelling at her. She did the same thing all of you would have done. The only difference is no one will ever see her coming…because no one really knows what she is capable of."

Aaron told Victor that Alyssa was right and any of them would have done the same. John and Stefano told Victor they had to let me grow up, because I wasn't a little girl they had to protect anymore.

Victor and Buono left with Stefano heading back to the plane to go back to Italy. Stefano called Jayce to let him know Victor and Buono had taken Vinnie's body back to Italy with them.

Jayce told me that Victor was going to personally deliver Vinnie's body to Naples along with Ponzio.

When I asked my husband who they were going to say killed Vinnie–he said that Victor was going take care of it, whatever that meant...

Chapter 13

June arrived to find we had enjoyed four peaceful months in a row.

Life was perfect, CJ and AJ were now crawling getting into everything and talking non-stop...

CJ's first words were mama and dada followed by gun! He would point and let us know every time he saw one now. At first it was when he would see mine and Jayce's, as well as the rest of the members in our clan.

Later he and AJ only said gun when it was someone they didn't know.

This of course came in handy, since the kids seemed to see everything.

Jayce and Ben thought it was funny at first. But we had come to realize it became quite helpful–since he kept Ben from getting shot when a hit-man tried to kill him.

Ben looked up as soon as my son said "gun"; killing the hit-man just before he fired at them.

Ben is a great shot and I know he will protect CJ, but I was not happy a hit-man almost killed my son.

Ben went out the next day and bought CJ a gun of his own.

I was just thankful it was only a toy! Of course it is now CJ's favorite toy and he carries it everywhere.

On the morning of my 18th birthday–CJ woke me up patting me on the cheek, "Mama… up… up… up!"

I opened my eyes looking at him as he clapped and giggles spilled from his lips.

He began crawling over to me as I stood up, holding out his arms for me to pick him up.

We found Jayce in the kitchen cooking breakfast and I put CJ down on the floor to play. Jayce turned around smiling at me as I walked over to get a cup of coffee.

"Happy Birthday, Angel! CJ wake you up?"

I just laughed as I told him how CJ woke me.

Jayce began telling me about the rabbits CJ had seen out in the front yard playing.

Hearing this CJ turned to look at me before he started crawling toward the window as he told me, "Mama… hop, hop, hop!"

I followed him as he crawled over to the window pointing to where the bunnies were playing–hopping over each other as they ran back and forth. CJ just smiled and laughed as he watched the rabbits playing.

Victor had called earlier this morning, before I woke up to let Jayce know he and the others had arrived to Angel Crest Estate.

Stefano had planned to have my party at the estate.

It is custom dating back generations, for the elder to hand over the Head of Family position, in a celebration on the heir's eighteenth birthday…by the giving of the Clan ring.

I was already Head of the Family for both Costa and Stefano's estate, but Stefano had insisted on still having the ceremony.

After we had eaten breakfast and gotten CJ dressed, we left to head to Angel Crest Estate.

Ben had come over just after Jayce finished cooking and ate breakfast with us. Ben was riding over with us so he could play with CJ, before we left and on the way.

Angel Crest Estate was filled with our entire clan-here to celebrate my eighteen birthday.

Stefano gave me my clan ring but mine was different from the others.

Jayce, Aaron and Nick's ring were all the same black onyx-with the Sicilian Clan emblem imbedded in the stone.

My ring was different. My father and the other elders had it made shortly after my birth.

The small box that Stefano took from his pocket before he handed to me…

I noticed right away it was one of the things I had taken from Haven Manor; when White Feather had killed my parents.

The ring was shaped into a crown, with the black onyx in the center and small pink diamonds at the top.

Victor and John both cried as Stefano slipped the ring on my right ring finger-the same finger all the others wore theirs on.

John had placed the mahogany box I had found hidden inside my bed on the table beside Stefano.

I asked Victor and the other about the box…

They only told me it wasn't time.

Victor had taken the ring placing it on top of the box, before turning and addressing everyone in the room.

"Today we celebrate Arabella's 18th birthday…as well as the giving of the Clan ring. She is now of age, just like the ones before her, we now pledge our lives to her."

I thought it was kind of strange, the whole ceremony; but Jayce and my brother said it was the same way with theirs.

We had just finished the ceremony…

John had just walked in the house to take the wooden box back inside as gun shots began to rain down on us.

I grabbed my gun in one hand and CJ in the other, as I shot back at the three men approaching.

Victor and the others were shooting trying to give us enough cover to get the kids back in the house.

I could see White Feather, along with three men advancing toward us.

Jayce and Nick both fired, taking two of the men down before Victor killed the other.

Seeing the three men dead beside him…

White Feather turned and disappeared along the tree line.

Victor and the others went after him…

They came back about an hour later, but…

White Feather was gone.

When Alyssa asked if he was coming back…

Victor only shook his head.

"No he's gone now. The box is secure there is no way for him to get it now."

Victor and the other elders refused to answer any questions, when we demanded to know what was inside the box. Victor wouldn't even tell us what it was that was so important, that White Feather was after it.

I watched Nick, Jayce and my brother fight with the elders…

Before long the three of them stormed out and left beyond angry.

They walked outside and started shooting in the same direction White Feather had gone.

Jayce and the guys came back in after they had calmed down, but the three of them refused to talk to John or Victor.

I knew Jayce was mad as hell, that CJ had been put in danger.

But he was beyond furious with Victor for not telling us what White Feather was after.

We all left Angel Crest Estate not long after the guys came back inside.

Ben had already took CJ and had him buckled in the car seat when Jayce came walking back in the house.

Later that night after we had put CJ to bed, Jayce and I sat up in bed talking.

I told Jayce, "I don't know what is inside that box....the one that Victor and the others keep hidden. All I know is, if White Feather threatens CJ over that damn box...well...Victor and the others better pray I don't kill them. It's a good thing that Victor left to go back to Italy this afternoon. I don't know what Nick is going to do. He is furious with Victor! Hopefully Francesca can keep him from killing his father on the plane. I just hope when they finally tell us all what the damn thing is that it doesn't get a bullet put in them!"

Life finally calmed back down, although Jayce, Aaron and Nick still refused to speak with any of the elders.

The party we had for the boys' first birthday; as well as Nick, Jayce and Aaron's 21st birthday–was a little uncomfortable with them not speaking. But, at least the kids had a great time.

We shot fireworks since we decided to have the party on July 4th this year. At least the fireworks were the only bang–not Jayce, Nick or Aaron shooting any of the elders. Although, I was on edge the entire time just waiting for something to go wrong.

Lily and Larson had found out they were expecting just two days after her 18th birthday. The baby was due around Valentine's Day. They both surprised us with the news, just before we shot the fireworks!

After the party was over, Jayce and the guys planned to meet up next morning with Nick and Nico...for a man/boys day they called it.

Whatever that means...I didn't mind since I had a list of things to do at home.

Victor and Nick had a meeting scheduled for July 7th they couldn't change, so they were leaving tomorrow night at seven to head back to Italy.

The guys were going to spend as much time tomorrow together as they could. We weren't sure how long before we got together again...especially with the guys not talking to the elders.

I had never seen them go this long without talking.

This time none of them would back down.

The elders refused to tell any of us what was in the locked mahogany wooden box...the one I had found hidden inside the frame of my bed, two years ago when White Feather killed my parents.

The box itself had gotten several people killed over the years. But putting our son, AJ and Nico in danger was completely different; and Jayce and the others saw it as an act of war.

Jayce, Nick and Aaron wanted to know, as Heads of the Family, they were entitled to know. They told the elders this but it made no difference.

We all thought that White Feather was after the box, but the elders wouldn't confirm or deny.

The elders refused to talk. The only thing that was said made even less sense.

Victor talked in riddles which only made the guys furious and left me with more questions that they wouldn't answer.

The only thing Victor told all of us was that we would get answers on the babies christening ceremony.

But that was six months away!

If this continued on for six more months with the guys and the elders; I was likely to shoot one of them for my own sanity.

I worry the kids christening ceremony will be an armed bomb just waiting…ticking…

I was also worried when we found out what it was…

Well, I can't imagine it is a good secret; those don't usually get people murdered.

The morning after the party I woke up just in time to tell CJ and Jayce good-bye.

Ben and Gage waved from the drive way as they climbed in with Jayce.

I had no clue what all of them were going to do but I knew they would be safe. Every one of them was armed with the exception of CJ, AJ and Nico.

I wouldn't be surprised, if the kids had their toy guns with them; or that one of the guys went to the store and bought some.

They all love to spoil the kids; and they all believe in always carrying a gun, no matter what kind (toy or real)!

I had just finished putting up the laundry and had walked in the kitchen for something to drink, when the doorbell started ringing.

I opened the front door to find Buono standing on my front porch. I was surprised to see him since I thought he was with Victor at the winery.

"Arabella, I thought I would visit you," Buono said as he walked by me into the house.

I knew there was a reason behind this visit; but I was always happy to see Buono.

We walked in the living room and sat down; after I had fixed him a drink.

I sat on the couch to get comfortable, seeing as I knew he was nervous. I had never seen Buono nervous to talk to me before and I wasn't sure whether to be scared or intrigued.

"Buono what's going on? Why are you so nervous? Did something happen?"

I asked trying to be patient as I sat waiting for him to talk.

He looked over at me and seemed to make up his mind to talk…but I couldn't figure out about what.

"Arabella first let me say that no one knows I am here. Victor and the others…this silent treatment and murderous glares they are giving each other…something has to give. I don't agree with Victor, John and Stefano about not telling you about the box and what it is. I won't tell you either…so don't ask, it is not my place to tell you.

Victor and the others are telling you the truth; you will find out about it in January but knowing Victor the answers you get will probably leave you with more questions. All of them are good with mind games…it's what makes them so good at destroying the enemy. The boys are just as bad…they learned from their fathers after all.

Arabella I believe if I explain what I can to you…you will be able to talk to the boys. Victor can never know what I tell you! But I can see it wearing on him, all this fighting with his son."

I wasn't sure what to say…

I was so shocked Buono was even telling me this. Victor would have a fit if he knew Buono was here. I knew it was hard for

Buono to go against Victor's wishes, so I knew whatever he had to tell me was important enough for him to go behind Victor's back.

I gave him my word I wouldn't say anything to Victor, John or Stefano. I agreed this couldn't continue on for six more months...

"Just tell me what you can Buono. I won't say anything to anyone, you don't want me to. I will try to talk to the guys but you know I can't make any promises that they will listen."

Buono shook his head at me...

"Arabella that is where you are wrong; the boys do listen to you. You have more power over them than you realize. They will listen because they know you have their best interest at heart. Princess...you are strong and you have compassion that will help you more than you can imagine.

I have watched you grow up. We never realized you would turn out to be our greatest treasure and our greatest weapon. Alyssa was right about no one really knowing what you are capable of. Princess...all of the elders along with the rest of us agree that you will be the change the clan has needed."

"I don't understand...what does that mean...that I will be the change," I asked Buono confused as to what they elders thought I would be.

"The box that was hidden...the same one the boys and elders are fighting over, it was locked for a reason. All I can tell you is this. The box will be given to you and only you...men for generations have killed for the contents of that box.

Your grandfather along with Victor and the others' fathers...became blood-thirsty over the power that box holds. Victor and the other elders locked the box shortly after they took over the clan; going legit as a way to keep history from repeating.

But the box's contents can only be given to someone who doesn't crave power…who will only use what's inside with a level head and heart. You Arabella, are the one…you were chosen, love.

White Feather wants the box; all of you are right about that. He has killed for what's inside and will continue until he has the box or he is dead. I am going with dead…he should have been dead long before now, but I have a feeling his time is coming.

You see Arabella…Victor will not tell the boys what they want to know. Not until the box is given to you. Those boys love you and they would never hurt you. When the box is yours…they will do whatever is needed to keep you safe and happy. They will never turn on you and together the six of you will be unstoppable."

I was stunned as I sat there not sure what to say. I knew the guys would never turn on me, I never thought they would.

But, Buono was talking like; I would need all five of them…to survive whatever was coming over this box! That didn't sound like a good secret to me, not at all!

I promised Buono I would talk to the Jayce and Nick.

Buono hugged me and kissed my forehead before he left, telling me to call if I needed anything.

I was sitting in the living room still trying to grasp everything Buono had told me, when Jayce and the others came in the living room.

Jayce came and sat down with CJ, before he asked if I was ok. I wasn't sure how to even answer him, as Nick and Aaron looked at me.

I looked at the three of them sitting there and then over at Ben and Gage.

"Guys I need to ask you something and...well I don't know how to explain it. I know you all love me and...well..." I stopped talking, not sure what to say.

"Princess of course we love you. What's going on," Nick asked as he sat Nico on the floor.

Aaron put AJ down next to Nico and CJ; the boys crawled over to CJ's toy box and started playing.

"Guys I need you to stop this silent argument you have going on with the elders. I know why you are mad...but I can't deal with this another six months. So for me...will you all please let it go for now?"

I waited until they all agreed; thankful I didn't need to give any reasons for my request. I would tell Jayce, Aaron and Nick about Buono's visit, just not today. I needed time to try and come to terms with what I learned.

If history kept repeating like Buono said, I was determined not to let it happen again.

I would keep all of them safe, even from themselves.

Chapter 14

Victor, Buono and Francesca were waiting by the plane as we dropped of Nick and Nico.

I was proud of Jayce and Aaron when they walked over and shook Victor's hand. Telling him it was time to pull together and not fight against each other.

Nick even shook his father's hand, telling him he meant no disrespect.

Buono was smiling at me so much that Victor asked me if I had anything to do with the change of heart they guys had. I only told him I had decided that I had had enough of their fighting and was calling a truce.

The next day Jayce and Aaron made peace with Uncle John and Stefano.

I could tell Ben knew there was something I wasn't telling them but he never asked. For that I was relieved and thankful.

July passed much more calmly now that everyone was on good terms.

Ben and Gage's 19th birthday party turned out even better than we could have ever hoped.

Doc's daughter Suzanna had moved to Paradise Falls to live.

I had met Suzanna when we were younger; but she lived with her mother and we didn't get to see each other often. She had just turned eighteen in February and had left to come live here with her dad.

Gage had fell in love at first sight...

Suzanna was still unsure, as to how to handle Gage's attention.

She knew what and who our family was, but she also knew we protected who we loved.

Gage, well he loved hard and fast. He didn't take kindly to not getting what he wanted and he wanted Suzanna.

I told Gage he had to slow down. He couldn't expect to run off with her and get married just because he wanted to. It took a lot of convincing before he finally realized he was going to have to win her over.

I blamed Jayce. I told him he was setting a bad example for Gage and Ben. Just because he told me at birth I would marry him; the rest of the world didn't work that way.

He just laughed and told me it should.

Gage and Suzanne were inseparable by the end of September.

I was worried Ben would feel left out not having Gage to pal around with...but of course that didn't happen.

If Gage and Ben weren't together, Ben was with me or off playing with CJ. He and CJ had gotten even closer over the past few months; they even had sleepovers on my living room floor.

I asked Ben one day; if we should find him a girl but he just looked at me and laughed as he asked me, "Why? I have you and you are enough. I don't need a woman telling me what to do. You already do that Princess!"

I just shook my head at Ben and didn't bring it up again.

I figured when the time was right Ben would find the right one and fall in love. I looked forward to meeting the girl that would steal Ben's heart away.

We all flew to Italy in October to celebrate Stefano's birthday and were staying for two weeks.

Victor and John insisted the boy's christening on January 6th take place in America. They didn't want to take any chances having it at the chapel in Italy.

The elders had built Angel's Wings Chapel in the center of all the towns. The vineyard workers and residents of all four towns used the chapel, especially for christening and sometimes weddings.

We had planned to do the boys' christening there, even though I wanted them to be christened in the same chapel as their fathers.

Victor thought it wasn't safe and I knew it was hard for him to back to place his wife was murdered.

Jayce and Aaron wanted to invite Ponzio, Gerardo and Federigo from the Rosarno Clan to the christening. Jayce, Aaron and I had become close to Ponzio.

I wasn't sure if anyone else from the Rosarno clan was coming, but I knew no one from the Camorra would be invited or even welcome.

We would have the entire Sicilian Clan at the christening or what is left of our family. Without my father and Costa there, it wouldn't seem complete.

We all left and flew back home the second week in November.

Alyssa and I finished planning everything for the christening; just in time for Thanksgiving.

We all had Thanksgiving together at Angel Crest Estate.

Victor, Buono, Nick, Nico and Francesca had flown in from Italy for the day. They could only stay for the day but were coming back to stay at least two weeks in December.

December seemed to be here before we knew it…

CJ, AJ and Nico were all walking and talking. It was more work to keep them out of the presents under the tree, than anything else.

Victor and the others flew in from Italy on December 18th and were planning to stay until after the christening.

Nick, Francesca and Nico stayed at Grey Crest Manor with Ben. Victor and Buono were staying with Stefano at Angel Crest Manor.

Francesca and Nico stayed with me at Legacy Meadows during the day while the guys worked.

Alyssa and AJ spend the days with us; letting the three boys play together.

Lily at seven months pregnant was fascinating to the boys; since they spent most of the time trying to talk to the baby and laughing, every time she kicked their hands.

On Christmas morning we all woke up to a white Christmas.

The boys wanted to play in the snow after they opened their presents.

The guys were just as bad–I'm not sure who started the snow fight, Jayce, Aaron or Nick. Ben and Gage weren't much better. All five of them were throwing snow balls at each other and running round and round the house, like five year olds!

Suzanna and Doc joined us at Angel Crest Manor for Christmas dinner. Gage surprised all of us when he asked Suzanna to marry him.

Benito and Doc were already talking about grandchildren.

Gage had taken Suzanna to carve their names in our tree Christmas Eve night after they left our house.

The morning of the christening the ground was still covered in snow.

I had just finished dressing CJ when Ben knocked on the front door. Nick, Francesca and Nico were riding over to the chapel with Aaron.

CJ went running to Ben as he bent down waiting with his arms opened. I left them playing and went to finish getting dressed myself.

Jayce had just finished buttoning his shirt when I walked back in our bedroom. I told him to keep an eye on Ben. I had seen the candy sticking out of Ben's pocket and I knew he would give CJ some.

When we loaded up in the car to head to the chapel; I knew CJ was on his second or third lollipop and I told Ben that was enough.

Ben just smiled at me, as he opened another lollipop sticking in his mouth.

We pulled in front of the chapel and Ben took CJ out the car and started inside.

Lily was coming in behind us but when she saw CJ's face covered in candy, she took him from Ben to go clean him up. Ben just smiled at her when he told her he didn't know how it had happened.

I was standing at the front of the chapel beside Jayce talking to the priest. Lily was still with CJ in the bathroom trying to wipe the candy off his face that Ben had given him.

Alyssa and Francesca were standing beside the priest; as he explained how the christening would be done. Alyssa and Francesca both were holding AJ and Nico in their arms...both boys turned and watched John and Stefano walking toward us.

Stefano was holding the mahogany box in his hands as he walked over and sat it down on the table in front of the priest.

I looked at Uncle Stefano smiling and asked him, "So...are you finally going to tell us what is in the box today?"

I never let on to the elders that Buono had talked to me. I never even got around to telling the guys, since I wasn't sure what to tell them. I knew they would have questions that I couldn't answer. I was also a little worried given what Buono had told me.

Buono had been right when he said the guys would protect me but I would protect them too.

He looked up at me smiling, "Yes, Arabella it is the..."

Stefano stopped talking as he reached for his gun looking behind me.

I heard the sound that made my heart stop as my son cried out to me.

I turned around with Jayce beside me and saw White Feather holding Lily and CJ, with a gun pointed at my son's head.

Before I could move White Feather turned and looked over at me.

"If you move Arabella I will kill your son first. Now I want all guns on the table and everyone to have a seat, now!"

I could hear Ponzio and Federigo behind me telling White Feather there was no way they would give up their guns.

White Feather just ignored them as he turned back to look at me.

"Princess I suggest you tell them to do as I say or I can shoot your son now, instead of later."

I looked at Victor beyond furious with him–as I told all of them to put their guns on the table and sit down.

Victor nodded at me; the same time as Ponzio and Federigo ask me if I was crazy.

Jayce looked over at Ponzio and Federigo.

"I suggest you both listen to my wife. You really don't want to piss her off right now…any more than she already is."

I didn't see the look Jayce gave them that had them bring their guns to the table and sitting down.

I never took my eyes off White Feather, as he continued to stare back at me.

Once everyone had sat down I still remained standing; only now the table beside me was now covered in guns.

White Feather told me to sit down too.

I just stood there staring at him, as fire seemed to burn all along my veins.

"No I think I'll stand. Since you have unarmed every man in here, there is no one left to shoot you. Now let my son go...get your gun away from his head. Let Lily and my son sit down with my husband. You can point your gun at me."

He looked over and saw how Jayce, Nick and Aaron reacted, when I told him to point the gun at me.

White Feather seemed to like the response he had gotten; as he let Lily take CJ over to Jayce.

I looked over at CJ and smiled at him as he sat in Jayce's lap watching White Feather and me.

I prayed that when I picked up a gun CJ wouldn't call out, "Mommy shoot!" like he always does now; when I hold one that isn't mine.

I looked at Jayce and nodded my head to CJ–he nodded back telling me he understood.

I hoped Jayce could keep him quiet.

I prayed this went like I hoped it would and we all walked out of here alive. I was worried something would happen today but I never expected this!

I was having a hard time not killing White Feather along with every elder in the room.

They should have told us the truth long before now.

Jayce, Nick and Aaron had done a good job making sure White Feather believed they were upset by what I said. I can always count on them backing whatever game I chose to play.

I noticed Ponzio and Federigo watching us and everything I did – as if they knew there was something going on.

I hoped when they left–they would leave seeing I truly am capable of being heir and just a small glimpse of what I really am capable of doing.

White Feather was going to die...

But he would now die by my hands for threatening CJ.

I looked at White Feather as I asked him, what it was he really wanted.

Since the elders refused to tell us–I hoped he would be more forthcoming with information.

"I want the box and to finish what I started. I failed to get it before but I won't this time. I didn't to kill Jayce, Nick and Aaron before at their christening but I won't fail to kill them now. I will wipe out the entire Sicilian Mafia line and everyone else that gets in my way. It seems only fitting that it started with three little baby boys and it will end with three little baby boys dead...along with their fathers. It seems almost poetic doesn't it? Any more questions Princess?"

I just looked at him as I nodded, "Yes I have one question. Since you are going to kill all of us; I just have one request, if you please?"

I waited hoping he would say yes without asking what I wanted.

He just looked at me and laughed, "Well, I don't see why not. Sure what would you like?"

I so badly wanted to laugh but I just looked at him as I laid my hand on the table, running my fingers over the guns.

I made my face look very sad as I told him, "You see I thought my father was best shooter there was but you proved me wrong when you killed him. I have to say, I was impressed I had never seen anyone best him."

I looked up as he smiled. I could tell it was working I almost had him where I wanted.

I just shrugged my shoulders as I continued to talk, still running my fingers over the guns on the table beside me.

"You know what I think is unfair? I can't help it I was born a girl. Everyone think I'm so weak. It makes me mad you know? Do you know what it feels like when people think you are weak...aren't afraid of you? My father was one of the most feared men in Italy and I have his blood running through my veins just like my brother."

I saw White Feather turn looking at Aaron, as I looked over facing my brother.

I could see Jayce out the corner of my eye nod his head at me, to keep going.

"You know what else is so bad? Even though his blood flows thru me; nobody fears me just because I am a girl. People fear you...did you know that? Did you know I have been afraid of you since I was a child," I asked him as he looked over at me smiling.

"Well no, I can't say I understand how you feel. People have always feared me. I'm not sure how to help you with that, Arabella."

That is exactly what I wanted to hear–as I looked up at him with a hopeful expression, "Well there is one thing. I would like to hold a gun just once. I have seen my husband hold his gun and I have always wanted to touch it. He won't let me touch it…all I want to do is just hold it one time."

I ran my hand over Jayce's gun, as I picked it up off the table holding it in my hand.

It wasn't my gun…

But he would find it poetic I'm sure.

White Feather just watched me as I looked at the gun in my hand. I could tell he really thought I had no idea what to do with it.

I watched as he lowered his gun by his side as he stood relaxed, watching me hold Jayce's gun in my hand.

I was so thankful that CJ had kept quiet as I turned to look over at him. It was almost like CJ knew not to make a sound.

Nico and AJ were quiet too, as they watched me.

I held the gun still studying it, as I noticed Ponzio and Federigo lean forward staring never taking their eyes from me.

I looked back up at White Feather as I raised the gun; still pretending to studying it as I began to talk.

"You know what I think is funny?"

I ask him as he looked at me and told me no.

I could tell he was listening to me. I had his complete attention.

"I think it's funny when people make assumptions about people they don't even know. I also think it is funny when people think they can threaten my family and they assume I will run. Most women would run, but like I said before I have Carmin Marcello blood in my veins. Did you know that when people look at me they see this little weak girl…not who I really am?"

He just looked at me and laughed, "Well, why don't you just tell them that you aren't weak? Just tell them you feel strong even though you can't shoot like your father. It doesn't really make you weak."

I just looked at him getting bored–I was ready to hold my son, play time was over.

I kept moving the gun around while I talked.

"You know what I think you are right. It is time to tell the truth. So let me tell you…there is something you don't know about me. You are right when you said I can't shoot like my father…" I looked over at Victor and smiled, as he smiled back at me.

I raised the gun so it was now pointed at White Feather but he still stood just watching me curiously, with his gun down by his side.

I was furious with him–as well as the elders. It was taking all I had to not shoot every one of them. I looked over at Victor before I turned back to White Feather.

I was gripping Jayce's gun in my hand and my finger was just itching to squeeze the trigger.

"You come in here on my son's christening and threaten him with a gun. You were right when you said this started with three baby boys and will end with three baby boys. Just not the way you think. I may not be able to shoot like my father or Victor, or any of the others. But, here's a secret you don't know…you will never see me coming because I was taught by the best…" I said as I fired the gun the bullet hitting him dead between the eyes.

He never even had time to lift his gun as the shot hit taking him to the floor.

I turned and looked at over at Victor. I could see Ponzio and Federigo sitting behind him, stunned as they looked back at me.

I had just killed the one man that had been untouchable…

The one man that was said to be untouchable and had personally killed more members of the Sicilian Mafia Clans, than any other.

I looked over at Victor as I pointed Jayce's gun at him and demanded, "What is in the box, Victor?"

He stood as he walked over placed his hand on the top of the box, before picking it up and handing it to me.

I reached for the box and tried to open it…

Only to find it still locked.

I looked up at Victor trying to keep from killing him for answers. I knew Victor liked his head games but this really wasn't the right time. I took a breath trying to calm down. As much as I wanted to demand he tell me what I wanted to know, I had been raised to respect Victor and the others.

"It's locked, Uncle Victor. Where is the key?"

Victor walked over to stand in front of me taking the gun from my hand and laying it on the table. He placed his hand on my cheek, as he smiled down at me.

"Arabella, this is the Mafia Bible and it is now yours. You will find the key hidden where your heart lives. Don't worry now Principessa. All will be answered in time. You will find it and when you do...Arabella, you will be the most powerful heir the Mafia has ever seen..."

Buono was right... more questions than answers...

But I would find the answers...

No, we would find the answers together...

All six of us together as a family...

Only I didn't know what would happen when we did...

I turned to reach for CJ...

The end?